Robert Alexander

Deception Over Edinburgh – Part Two

Contents

Recap of Book 1: Shadows Over Edinburgh

In Shadows Over Edinburgh, Detective Horace MacLeod teams up with tech savvy hacker Aidan Fraser and journalist Evelyn Reid to investigate a series of mysterious disappearances linked to the secretive Obsidian Order. The investigation uncovers a dark conspiracy rooted in Edinburgh's history. As the trio delves deeper, they face numerous dangers, including betrayal from within and violent confrontations. The book ends with the protagonists narrowly escaping death, but the Obsidian Order remains at large, its full extent still hidden.

Recap of Book 2: Deception Over Edinburgh – Part One

Deception Over Edinburgh continues the story as Horace, Evelyn, and Aidan deal with the aftermath of their earlier investigation. They discover that the Obsidian Order's influence reaches further than they initially thought, with ties to powerful international entities. The tension escalates as the trio faces new threats and internal conflicts. Horace's leadership is tested, Evelyn uncovers deeper layers of corruption, and Aidan struggles with his personal demons. The book concludes with a shocking twist, leaving the characters in a state of uncertainty and the conspiracy unresolved.

Character Bios

Horace MacLeod: A determined and seasoned detective, Horace is driven by a strong moral code and a desire to see justice served. His experience and instincts make him a natural leader, but his relentless pursuit of the truth often puts him in dangerous situations.

Evelyn Reid: A passionate and courageous journalist, Evelyn is committed to uncovering the truth, no matter the personal cost. Her investigative skills and determination have made her a key player in the fight against the Obsidian Order, though her tenacity sometimes leads her into perilous situations.

Aidan Fraser: A brilliant but troubled hacker, Aidan's technical expertise is invaluable to the team. However, his past and personal struggles, including a battle with addiction, complicate his role in the investigation. Aidan is constantly grappling with his sense of identity and loyalty.

Sophie Dawson: A character connected to Aidan, Sophie's role is more personal, intertwining with the main characters in ways that complicate their mission. Her motivations and actions have a significant impact on the storyline, especially in her interactions with Aidan.

James Dyer: A journalist with connections to the media, James plays a crucial role in spreading information and influencing public perception. His decisions and actions have far-reaching consequences, particularly in relation to the investigation and the main characters.

Prologue

The night air was thick with the scent of rain-soaked earth as Donovan Cross moved silently through the abandoned warehouse on the outskirts of Edinburgh. The only sound was the soft scuff of his polished shoes against the concrete floor. The Raven had many places like this—hidden corners of the city where their business could be conducted away from prying eyes.

Ahead, a single overhead light flickered, casting eerie shadows that danced along the rusted walls. In the centre of the room, a man was bound to a chair, his head slumped forward, blood dripping from a gash on his temple. Donovan's eyes narrowed as he approached, his gaze cold and calculating.

The man's face, though bruised and bloodied, was still recognizable—Mark Lawson. Mark had been a low-level operative in The Raven's organization, a courier who had once carried sensitive messages and packages through the city's labyrinthine streets. He had managed to stay under the radar, always keeping his head down and doing as he was told. But recently, Mark had made the fatal mistake of thinking he could bargain with the police, trading information for immunity.

"Mark," Donovan's voice was smooth, almost soothing, as he stepped closer. "Do you know why you're here?"

Mark's head lifted slightly, his swollen eyes filled with terror. He tried to speak, but all that came out was a strangled gasp, the pain overwhelming his ability to form coherent words. Donovan crouched down, bringing himself to eye level with the trembling man.

"You had a good run, Mark," Donovan continued, his tone soft, almost paternal. "You were useful for a time. But you made a mistake, and now you have to pay for it."

Mark began to whimper, his voice barely audible. "Please... I didn't mean to... I was just scared—"

"Scared?" Donovan's voice shifted, a flash of anger igniting in his eyes. He straightened, towering over the man. "You think you're scared now? You haven't even begun to understand fear."

In an instant, Donovan's calm facade cracked. He lashed out, kicking the chair out from under Mark, sending him crashing to the floor with a thud. The sound echoed through the warehouse, a sharp contrast to the previous quiet.

"Did you think you could betray me and live?" Donovan snarled, his temper flaring. He grabbed Mark by the collar, dragging him upright, the man's legs scraping against the concrete. "Did you think The Raven would let you walk away?"

Mark tried to stammer out a plea, but Donovan silenced him with a backhanded slap, the force of the blow snapping Mark's head to the side. Blood dribbled from the corner of his mouth as he gasped for breath, his eyes wide with terror.

"You disgust me," Donovan hissed, his voice dripping with venom. "You're nothing. Just a snivelling, pathetic little worm who thought he could bite the hand that feeds him."

Donovan's grip tightened, his knuckles white with rage. He could feel the heat of his fury coursing through him, a fire that demanded to be quenched with blood. This wasn't just about punishment—it was about making sure that Mark, and anyone else who dared to think they could betray The Raven, understood the consequences.

"You were nothing, Mark. And now, you're less than nothing." Donovan released him, letting him slump back to the floor. He pulled a slender, silver knife from his coat, the blade gleaming in the dim light. He moved with lethal precision, the knife flashing in the air before plunging deep into Mark's chest.

Mark let out a choking cry, his body convulsing as Donovan twisted the blade, ensuring the wound would be fatal. Blood spilled onto the concrete, pooling beneath the chair, a dark reminder of the cost of crossing The Raven.

Donovan stepped back, his expression hard and unforgiving as he watched the life drain from Mark's eyes. There was no satisfaction in this, only the cold certainty that he had done what was necessary. The Raven demanded loyalty, and anything less was met with the harshest of consequences.

As Mark's breathing slowed, Donovan leaned in close, his voice a deadly whisper. "This is what happens to those who think they can outsmart us. You were nothing, and now you're less than nothing."

He wiped the blade clean on Mark's shirt before slipping it back into his coat. But as he did, his mind was already turning over the next steps. Mark wasn't the only one who had shown disloyalty recently—there were others, and Donovan intended to root them all out. He wouldn't stop until every last one of them had been dealt with, until The Raven was purged of any weakness.

The fire in Donovan's chest still burned as he walked away. As he reached the warehouse's entrance, he paused, his eyes catching sight of an old oil can lying against the wall. A slow, wicked smile spread across his face. He kicked the can over with a casual flick of his foot, the thick liquid spilling out across the floor, spreading toward the centre of the room where Mark's lifeless body slumped.

Donovan reached into his pocket and pulled out a matchbook, his fingers steady as he struck a match. The small flame danced for a moment before he turned and, with a final glance at the carnage he had wrought, tossed the lit match over his shoulder.

The match arced through the air, landing in the spreading pool of oil. There was a brief, almost eerie silence before the flames erupted, quickly consuming the oil and licking up the walls of the warehouse. The fire spread rapidly, feeding off the dry wood and old chemicals stored in the building. Within moments, the entire room was ablaze, the heat intense and suffocating.

Donovan didn't look back as the flames roared to life. He strode out of the warehouse, the heat from the fire warming his back as he moved through the night. The building behind him was a silhouette of destruction, flames licking at the sky, smoke billowing into the air in thick, black clouds.

He reached his car, a sleek, black sedan parked just outside the warehouse gates. The reflection of the inferno glimmered in the car's polished surface as Donovan opened the door and slid into the driver's seat. The sound of the roaring fire was muffled as he shut the door, the world outside silenced as if nothing had happened.

Donovan adjusted the rearview mirror, catching a glimpse of the warehouse engulfed in flames. The structure groaned under the heat, beams collapsing as the fire consumed everything within. It was a fitting end for a traitor—a cleansing fire that would leave nothing but ash in its wake.

With a flick of his wrist, Donovan started the engine. The car purred to life, and he pulled away from the burning warehouse, his expression calm, almost serene. As he drove through the dark streets of Edinburgh, the orange glow of the fire slowly faded in his rearview mirror, leaving only the cold darkness of the night.

To Donovan, it was just another loose end tied up, another reminder of the price of betrayal. The fire behind him was a symbol—a message that The Raven was not to be trifled with. He had more work to do, more names to cross off his list. But for now, as he merged onto the main road, Donovan allowed himself a moment of satisfaction.

The night had been long, and the work had been bloody, but it was necessary. It was the price of power, and Donovan was more than willing to pay it.

As the city lights flickered in the distance, Donovan's thoughts turned to the future. There would always be those who challenged The Raven, those who thought they could defy him. But they would learn, just as Mark Lawson had learned tonight—no one crossed Donovan Cross and lived to tell the tale.

And with that, Donovan disappeared into the night, the weight of shadows following close behind.

CHAPTER ONE – THREE YEARS LATER

The events of this book take place three years after 'Deception Over Edinburgh – Part One'

Aidan

Aidan Fraser blinked against the sharp sunlight slicing through the half-drawn blinds of his apartment. The room, a monument to his slow-motion collapse, stank of stale alcohol and failure. His once meticulously groomed appearance had given way to neglect —greasy, unkempt hair hung in his eyes, and his clothes, stained and wrinkled, clung to him like a second skin. Empty bottles littered the floor, silent witnesses to the nights he'd rather forget and the days he couldn't face.

He sat up, his head pounding with the dull ache of a hangover. His fingers traced the scar on his right hand, a souvenir from his final battle with The Obsidian Order three years ago. That hand, once a symbol of his prowess—a hacker's hand that could slip into the most secure systems—now trembled, barely able to hold a bottle steady. Unwelcome memories flickered through his mind: the adrenaline, the fear, and the sickening realization of just how deep The Raven's influence had burrowed. He'd thought Horace's arrest would be their escape, a chance to start fresh with Sophie. Instead, the aftermath had dragged him down into a darkness he couldn't escape.

His phone buzzed—a rare sound these days. A message from an

old contact, someone who hadn't given up on him. It hinted at a job, something big enough to pull him out of this nosedive. Aidan stared at the screen, caught between the ghost of his old self and the bottle in his hand. He hadn't touched a keyboard in months, hadn't hacked anything more challenging than his TV for free cable. The lure of the digital underworld tugged at him, the promise of that familiar rush. But could he really dive back in after everything?

Sophie

Sophie stood on the edge of her balcony, gazing out over Edinburgh as the evening sun bathed the city in gold. Her rooftop apartment, dripping with luxury, was a reminder of The Raven's reach—every inch of it paid for in loyalty and secrets. But no amount of wealth could fill the emptiness gnawing at her. She swirled the wine in her glass, her thoughts far from the opulence around her. Inside, Clarice's laughter drifted through the glass doors, bittersweet and distant. Sophie's heart clenched at the thought of the life that might have been—her, Aidan, and their daughter, together. But that life was a dream, traded away for the cold comfort of survival.

Her phone buzzed, jolting her back to reality. The Raven. A reminder of the cost of all this. Sophie took a slow breath and answered, her voice calm while everything inside her quaked.

The voice on the other end was as icy and calculating as ever, issuing orders that felt more like chains. As the words flowed over her, Sophie's mind wandered back to the night she had first reached out to The Raven. Aidan had disappeared into another alcohol-soaked oblivion, and Clarice had been burning with fever. Desperation had driven her to make that call—a betrayal of Aidan, of herself. The help came quickly, too quickly, and with it, the invisible threads that bound her tighter to The Raven.

She had told herself it was for Clarice, that she had no other choice. But now, standing in this gilded cage, Sophie couldn't shake the doubt that clawed at her. The voice on the phone droned on, cold and commanding, and she knew she would obey. But as she hung up, a chill crept through her, settling deep in her bones. How much longer could she keep living this lie?

Evelyn

In the suffocating gloom of her basement flat, Evelyn Reid hunched over her desk, a hollowed-out version of the woman she once was. The walls seemed to press in on her, thick with the stench of neglect and despair. Her hands, once steady, now trembled above a blank sheet of paper. Weeks had passed since she last tried to write—words slipping away, lost in the fog that clouded her mind.

She glanced at the remnants of her past scattered across the desk: a tattered notebook, yellowed clippings, a pen she couldn't bring herself to pick up. The voices in her head, cruel and relentless, whispered her failures, taunting her with who she used to be. She could still see it—the night everything shattered. Horace's frantic call, the dossier landing like a bomb on her doorstep, the police pounding at her door. It had all unravelled in hours—her career, her reputation—everything destroyed by one mistake.

Evelyn took a shaky breath, her chest tightening as tears threatened. Once, she had been strong, unstoppable even. Now, she was nothing. The press had hailed her as a hero, then branded her a pariah, and finally turned her into a cautionary tale. She hadn't seen Aidan in over a year, hadn't spoken to Sophie since the trial, and the thought of facing Horace, of making sense of it all, was unbearable. The spark that had driven her was gone, smothered by the weight of a world that no longer cared. She was alone, broken, and darkness was all she had left.

CHAPTER TWO
– THE CAGE

Horace MacLeod sat alone in the cold, grey cell that had been his home for three long years. The bare, unyielding walls seemed to press in on him, a constant reminder of the life he had lost. The clinking of keys and the distant murmur of other prisoners were the only sounds breaking the heavy silence. He ran his fingers over the rough surface of the small wooden table, tracing the grooves etched into it over time.

His mind wandered back to the trial—a spectacle that had captured the nation's attention. The prosecution had painted him as a traitor, a man who had used his position to aid The Raven, betraying the city he had sworn to protect. They had piled up evidence—financial records, encrypted messages, eyewitness accounts—all pointing to Horace as a key player in The Raven's operations. The charges were crushing: conspiracy to commit murder, racketeering, espionage, obstruction of justice, and treason. The jury had needed only a few hours to convict him —guilty on all counts.

The sentence had been swift and final: life in prison, no parole. Outwardly, Horace had taken it with the stoicism that defined his career, but inside, something had shattered. The weight of the accusations, the betrayal by those he trusted, and the knowledge that he had failed to protect his city, his friends, even himself—it was almost too much to bear.

Horace stood and walked to the small, barred window that offered a sliver of the outside world. The sky was a dull grey, mirroring the despair lodged deep within him. He had always prided himself on seeing through lies, uncovering the truth no matter how buried. But now, he was the one buried—beneath layers of deceit and betrayal. The question gnawed at him: had he been blind, or had someone orchestrated this fall, always one step ahead?

His thoughts drifted to Evelyn and Aidan. Over the years, he'd heard snippets—Evelyn's breakdown, Aidan vanishing into his own shadows. Guilt tugged at him, wondering if their fates were tangled with his. He had always been the protector, shielding others from harm. But in the end, he had failed them all.

A faint sound broke through his reverie—the jingle of keys, the heavy clank of a door unlocking. Horace turned to see a guard enter, tossing a small envelope onto the table before leaving without a word.

Horace stared at the envelope, his mind racing. He rarely received mail; who would write to him now? He picked it up cautiously, his fingers brushing the familiar handwriting. Margaret. A name from a lost past. The one person who had believed in him, even when he couldn't believe in himself.

With trembling hands, Horace opened the envelope. The letter inside was brief, but its words reignited something within him— something he had thought long dead. Margaret wrote of doubts, unanswered questions, a truth she believed still lingered out there, waiting to be uncovered. She urged him not to give up, to keep fighting, because there were still those who believed in him.

Horace sat back down, the letter clutched in his hand. The despair that had gripped him for so long loosened, just slightly. But he knew better than to let hope take root too easily. The forces against him were powerful, and he had been caught off guard before. Caution and pragmatism had kept him alive as a detective, and they would have to serve him now.

He folded the letter carefully, tucking it back into the envelope and placing it in the drawer. The possibility that Margaret might be onto something was worth considering, but he couldn't afford to act rashly. He needed to think, plan, and observe. The truth, if it was still out there, would require patience and precision.

As the sky darkened, Horace stared out of the small window. His situation was precarious, and any move he made had to be calculated. The game wasn't over, but he had to play it wisely. Hope was dangerous—but with caution, it might just become his weapon.

CHAPTER THREE: THE SHADOWS WE KEEP

Aidan Fraser stared into the cracked bathroom mirror, running a hand through his tangled hair. His reflection stared back at him, haggard and worn—eyes bloodshot, stubble too far gone to be considered anything close to stylish. He hadn't shaved in days, maybe weeks, and the man looking back at him was barely recognizable.

He reached for the scissors on the sink, the cold metal heavy in his hand. Cutting his hair was supposed to be a symbolic act, a step towards reclaiming some semblance of control. But even as he positioned the blades over a lock of hair, doubt crept in. Would this really change anything? Or was he just fooling himself?

His phone buzzed on the counter, cutting through the silence. He ignored it. Whoever it was, they weren't offering anything he wanted—nothing but trouble, reminders of a past he'd been trying to bury at the bottom of a bottle.

Aidan hesitated, scissors poised. He knew what he should do. Clean up. Get his life together. Be someone Sophie and Clarice could be proud of, even if they were no longer in his life. But the weight of his failures pressed down on him, suffocating.

He closed his eyes, letting the scissors drop back to the sink with a clatter. Who was he kidding? A haircut wasn't going to change the fact that he'd screwed everything up. It wasn't going to erase the disappointment in Sophie's eyes, the way she had looked at him the day of the crash.

He could still see it—the way her hands had gripped Clarice tightly in the back seat, her knuckles white as she tried to shield their daughter from the reality of who he was. The accident hadn't been serious, but it had been enough. Enough to break what little trust was left between them.

Aidan exhaled slowly, leaning heavily against the sink. "Come on, man," he muttered to himself. "Get it together."

But the pep talk fell flat. He wasn't that guy anymore—the one who could talk his way out of anything, the one who could pick himself up after a fall. That version of Aidan had disappeared a long time ago, buried under layers of guilt, shame, and whiskey.

His phone buzzed again, louder this time, as if demanding his attention. He finally picked it up, glancing at the screen. A message from an old contact, someone who had pulled him back into the digital underworld more times than he cared to admit.

Need your help. Big job. You in?

Aidan stared at the message, his mind racing. It was tempting—so damn tempting. The thrill of the hack, the rush of outsmarting the system—it had always been an escape for him. A way to forget, if only for a little while.

But what had it gotten him? A broken family, a shattered life, and the same damn mess staring back at him in the mirror.

He typed a quick response, his fingers trembling. *Not interested.* He hit send before he could change his mind.

The phone buzzed again almost immediately. *You sure? Could use a guy like you. Pays well.*

Aidan's hand clenched around the phone. The pull was strong, stronger than he wanted to admit. It would be easy to fall back into that world, to lose himself in the code, to forget about everything else.

But then he thought of Sophie and Clarice. Thought of the look on Sophie's face when she realized he wasn't the man she thought he was. Thought of the day he walked out of their lives because staying felt like he was doing more harm than good.

With a grunt, Aidan tossed the phone onto the counter and turned on the faucet. Cold water splashed over his face, shocking him back into the present. He needed to focus, to find a way out of the darkness that had consumed him for so long.

"Cut the damn hair," he muttered to himself, picking up the scissors again. But his hands were shaking now, and he couldn't bring himself to do it. He was frozen, caught between who he wanted to be and who he really was.

The silence in the apartment was deafening, and Aidan could feel the walls closing in on him. His gaze flicked to the bottle of whiskey sitting on the kitchen counter, its amber liquid glinting in the dim light. It would be so easy to give in, to drown it all out, to let the numbness take over.

Just one drink, he told himself. Just enough to take the edge off. But deep down, he knew better. One drink had never been enough.

He stalked over to the bottle, his hands trembling as he reached for it. The familiar weight of it in his hand was almost comforting. But as he unscrewed the cap, the smell of the alcohol hit him like a punch to the gut, and memories came flooding back—memories of Sophie, of Clarice, of everything he had lost.

He squeezed his eyes shut, his knuckles white as he gripped the bottle. "No," he whispered, more to himself than anyone else. "Not today."

But the temptation was too strong, and Aidan could feel himself slipping. His resolve was crumbling, and the only thing standing between him and the bottle was a thin thread of self-control that could snap at any moment.

"Don't do this," he muttered, his voice barely audible over the pounding of his heart. "You're stronger than this."

But was he? Was he really?

The phone buzzed again, pulling him out of his thoughts. Another message, another offer. He glanced at the screen, torn between the easy escape it promised and the crushing weight of his reality.

With a growl of frustration, Aidan hurled the bottle across the room. It hit the wall with a shattering crash, the whiskey spilling across the floor in a golden pool. The sound echoed in the empty apartment, and for a moment, Aidan just stood there, breathing heavily, his hands clenched into fists at his sides.

He felt a strange mix of triumph and defeat, as if he had won a battle but lost the war. The temptation was still there, gnawing at the edges of his mind, but he had resisted—barely.

Aidan sank onto the couch, burying his face in his hands. He was exhausted, both physically and mentally, and the thought of facing another day felt like an insurmountable task. But he knew he couldn't keep going like this. Something had to change.

His phone buzzed one last time, and Aidan picked it up with a sigh. The message was simple, just two words: *Your call.*

He stared at the screen for a long time, his thoughts a chaotic whirlwind of doubt, regret, and the faintest glimmer of hope. He had made it through today, but tomorrow was a different story. Aidan knew that he was standing on the edge of a precipice, one wrong step away from falling back into the abyss.

CHAPTER 4: BENEATH THE SURFACE

Sophie sank into the plush cushions of the couch, her eyes closing as the weight of her thoughts pressed down on her. The glass of wine in her hand had long gone warm, forgotten as her mind spiralled back to the choices that had led her here. The cool air drifting through the open balcony door did little to ease the tension coiling in her chest. She had everything she had once thought she wanted—luxury, security, power—but the emptiness gnawed at her, a hollow ache that only grew stronger with each passing day.

The apartment was immaculate, a pristine sanctuary high above the city, far removed from the grime and danger below. The Raven had given her this life—a gilded cage, perfect in every outward appearance. But Sophie could feel the bars tightening around her, closing off any chance of escape.

From the other room, she heard Clarice's laughter, bright and innocent. The sound echoed off the walls, bittersweet and painful. Sophie's heart twisted. That laugh, that joy, should have been enough. But it only reminded her of the life that could have been— if Aidan had been different, if she had been stronger, if she hadn't made the choices that now haunted her.

But that life was gone, buried beneath layers of deceit and necessity. Joining The Raven had seemed like the only option at the time, the only way to protect Clarice from the dangers that lurked in the shadows. At first, the power and security had been intoxicating, a heady rush that made her believe she could control her own destiny. But each day in this gilded cage, Sophie felt herself slipping further away from the woman she had once been.

Her phone buzzed on the coffee table, snapping her back to the present. She opened her eyes, her hand tightening around the glass of wine as she reached for the phone with the other. The number on the screen was familiar—a contact within The Raven, someone she had come to rely on, though she knew better than to fully trust them.

"Sophie," the voice greeted her when she answered, smooth and authoritative. The voice of someone who had all the power. "We need to discuss your next move."

Sophie swallowed hard, dread pooling in her stomach. "What is it?"

"There's a situation developing. We need you ready. Certain individuals require attention. You understand?"

The words were clinical, cold. Sophie nodded, even though the voice on the other end couldn't see her. "Yes, I understand."

"Good. I'll send you the details. And Sophie... remember where your loyalties lie."

The line went dead, the finality of the words ringing in Sophie's ears. She lowered the phone slowly, the weight of her choices pressing down harder than ever. The air in the apartment seemed to thicken, and she could feel the invisible chains binding her to this life, this role she had chosen for herself.

Too deep to turn back now. That's what she told herself every day, the mantra that kept her moving forward. But the path ahead was growing darker, and Sophie couldn't shake the feeling that she was walking deeper into a trap of her own making.

Clarice's voice called out from the other room, pulling Sophie from her thoughts. She set the phone down and made her way to her daughter, finding her playing on the floor, surrounded by toys. The sight brought a bittersweet smile to Sophie's lips. But reality pressed in. She couldn't stay. Not tonight.

Sophie sighed, running a hand through her hair as she pulled out her phone again. There was only one person she could call for help with Clarice tonight, even if it meant enduring the questions and the disapproving looks.

She dialled her mother's number, each ring sending a ripple of tension through her. Finally, her mother's voice answered, warm but cautious. "Sophie? Is everything alright?"

"Yes, Mum," Sophie replied, forcing cheerfulness into her voice. "I just—could you come over and watch Clarice tonight? Something's come up."

There was a pause on the other end, and Sophie could almost hear her mother's mind working. "You've been out a lot lately, Sophie. Are you sure everything's okay?"

Sophie closed her eyes, leaning against the wall. "It's just work, Mum. You know how it is."

Her mother's sigh was heavy, filled with the weight of unasked questions. "I'll be there in twenty minutes. But Sophie... we need to talk."

"Thanks, Mum. I really appreciate it." Sophie ended the call quickly, knowing the conversation would only get harder if it continued.

Twenty minutes felt like an eternity, but soon enough, there was a knock on the door. Sophie opened it to find her mother standing there, her expression a mix of concern and suspicion. Clarice ran up to her grandmother with a squeal of delight, and for a moment, the tension eased as her mother scooped the little girl into her arms.

"Hi, sweetie," her mother said, smiling at Clarice before turning her gaze back to Sophie. "Are you going to tell me what's really going on?"

Sophie stiffened, forcing a smile. "It's nothing, Mum. Just work. I won't be long."

Her mother's eyes narrowed slightly, scanning the pristine apartment, the luxurious surroundings that had appeared so suddenly in Sophie's life. "This work of yours... it's different from what you used to do, isn't it?"

Sophie's heart pounded in her chest. She had anticipated this conversation, dreaded it even, but she wasn't ready. "Mum, please. I really can't talk about it right now."

Her mother set Clarice down gently and stepped closer to Sophie, her voice soft but firm. "I know something's wrong, Sophie. You're not the same. You don't have to tell me everything, but... just be careful, alright? For Clarice's sake."

Guilt tightened in Sophie's chest, and she nodded, unable to meet her mother's eyes. "I will. I promise."

Her mother watched her for a moment longer, then nodded, stepping back. "Alright. Go on, then. I'll take care of Clarice."

"Thanks, Mum," Sophie whispered, grabbing her coat and heading for the door. The weight of her mother's words hung heavy over her as she stepped into the cool evening air. The Raven's expectations were already crushing, but now, the weight of her mother's concern added another layer to the burden.

As she walked away from the apartment, Sophie glanced back at the warm light spilling from the windows. Her mother was right —something was wrong. But Sophie didn't know how to fix it. All she could do was keep moving forward, even as the path grew darker and more treacherous.

Her phone buzzed again, another message from The Raven. Sophie stared at the screen for a long moment, her heart heavy with dread. But there was no turning back now.

With a sigh, she slipped the phone into her pocket and walked into the night, the city stretching out before her like a labyrinth she would never escape.

But for now, there was no other choice. She had to keep moving forward. It was the only thing she knew how to do.

CHAPTER 5: RESURRECTION

Evelyn Reid sat in the dim light of her basement flat, staring at the unopened notebook in front of her. Its pages were as blank as her prospects, and the irony wasn't lost on her. She traced the edge of the worn leather cover, a relic from when she thought she could change the world with a pen. Back when she was someone—respected, feared even—for her ability to unearth the truth. That life was long gone, swallowed up in the chaos she couldn't outrun.

Her fingers trembled as she lingered on the cover, and a wave of dizziness washed over her. She closed her eyes, waiting for the sensation to pass, reminding herself it was just the medication. Just the pills dulling the edges, taking the sharpness away. She was in control, she told herself, even as the world blurred around her.

The doctors had prescribed them for the anxiety, the nightmares that wouldn't let her sleep. At first, she'd taken them sparingly, afraid of losing the edge that had once made her formidable. But as the weight of everything pressed down on her—Horace's trial, the relentless media scrutiny, the isolation—she found herself reaching for the bottle more and more often.

One pill to take the edge off. Then another to silence the whispers that haunted her at night. Before she knew it, she was taking double the prescribed dose, convincing herself it was necessary, just to function. Just to keep going.

Evelyn opened her eyes, blinking against the dim light. The dizziness had passed, but the fog remained, a thick haze that dulled her senses. She knew she was losing her grip, slipping further away from reality with each passing day. But what did it matter? What did she have left to hold onto, anyway?

Her gaze drifted to the clippings scattered across the desk—ghosts of stories she had once chased with fervour. Names and faces stared back at her, some familiar, others fading into obscurity. Among them was Horace MacLeod, his photo from the day of his sentencing glaring up at her. His eyes, though dark and shadowed, still held a trace of the man she had known—a man betrayed by the very system he served.

Join the club, Horace, she thought bitterly. The world had turned on them both, chewed them up, and spit them out when they were no longer useful.

She picked up the photo, her fingers trembling. "We were supposed to be the good guys," she whispered to the empty room, her voice thick with bitterness. "We were supposed to make a difference."

But the world didn't care about good guys. It cared about narratives, about heroes and villains, and when the narrative didn't fit, it twisted you until you did. The headlines had once hailed her as a hero, a whistleblower who exposed the Obsidian Order. But that praise had a short shelf life. When the real battle began—when the truth became inconvenient—they turned on her, ripping apart the very foundation of her existence.

The media had branded her unstable, unreliable—a cautionary tale for anyone who dared dig too deep. The police, once her allies, had distanced themselves, and her contacts in the press? They stopped returning her calls faster than you could say "career suicide."

Evelyn laughed, a hollow, bitter sound that echoed through the empty flat. "Career suicide. That's one way to put it."

But deep down, she knew it was more than that. She hadn't just lost her career; she had lost herself. Piece by piece, the woman she used to be had been stripped away, until all that was left was this— a hollow shell, barely holding it together with medication and lies.

Her eyes drifted back to the notebook, still unopened on the desk. She knew she should write, should try to make sense of the chaos swirling in her mind. But the thought of putting pen to paper felt like an insurmountable task, a reminder of the woman she no longer was.

Still, something flickered within her—a faint echo of the resolve she once carried. She had let the world convince her she was finished, that she had nothing left to fight for. But looking at Horace's face, at the forgotten stories littering her desk, that old fire sparked to life. It was weak, barely a flicker, but it was there.

"I'm not done yet," she muttered, more to herself than anyone else. "Not yet."

She remembered the day they found the dossier on her doorstep, the one that led to Horace's downfall. The dread she had felt, knowing they were being played, that someone had orchestrated it all. But in the chaos that followed, the truth had been buried beneath layers of lies and deception. And she—well, she had been too broken, too distracted by her own unravelling, to see it through.

But now, sitting in her dingy flat, the pieces started to click into place. The dossier, the trial, the whispers that had haunted her—it all pointed to something she had missed. Something crucial. She could feel it, just beyond her reach. And this time, she wouldn't let it slip away—not without a fight, at least.

Evelyn reached for the bottle of pills on the edge of the desk, her fingers hovering over it. She stared at it for a long moment, the temptation strong. Just one more, she thought. Just enough to clear the fog, to help her focus. But something inside her resisted, a small voice reminding her that she was already teetering on the edge. Another pill, and she might not come back.

With a sigh, she pulled her hand away and grabbed the notebook instead. The pen felt heavier than it should, but she forced herself to write, slowly at first, then faster. Notes, questions, connections she hadn't seen before. Each word brought a spark of clarity, a thread to follow.

The hours slipped by unnoticed as she worked, the dim glow of the desk lamp her only companion. By the time she looked up, the notebook was half-filled with scrawled notes, diagrams, and fragments of ideas. It wasn't much, but it was more than she had done in months. Maybe she wasn't entirely useless after all.

She leaned back in her chair, exhaustion weighing on her, but for the first time in a long while, there was a sense of purpose. She wasn't the same woman she had been three years ago, but she wasn't finished yet. There was still truth to uncover, still a chance to make something right—even if she wasn't exactly sure what that looked like.

Evelyn glanced at Horace's photo one last time before closing the notebook. She didn't know what she would find, or if it would change a damn thing.

The world had labelled her a flake, an unstable relic of a forgotten battle. Maybe they were right. Maybe she was losing her grip.

As the fog threatened to close in again, Evelyn reached for the bottle of pills and shoved it into the drawer. Out of sight, out of mind. She wasn't ready to give up just yet. Not when there was still a chance—even a slim one—that she could make a difference.

cold, calculating place where he thrived. The Raven's operations were expanding, and his control over the city was tightening with every passing day. He would continue to pull the strings, ensuring that those who opposed him were silenced before they could even begin to rise.

Because in Donovan's world, there was no room for defiance. Power was absolute, and he intended to wield it until his enemies were nothing more than distant memories, crushed under the weight of his influence.

CHAPTER 7: A VOICE IN THE SHADOWS

James Dyer sat behind his sleek, polished desk, the office of his TV news channel humming with quiet efficiency around him. The view from his window overlooked the city of Edinburgh, a city that had changed little in appearance, but so much in its undercurrents since the fall of Horace MacLeod and the unravelling of Evelyn Reid's career. The past haunted him—whispers of a life before Donovan Cross, before the compromises that had chipped away at his integrity.

It was three years ago when everything started to shift. He remembered the day the anonymous dossier landed on his desk. He could still see the envelope, plain and unassuming, holding within it the power to change the course of lives. It was supposed to go to Evelyn, but fear and ambition drove him to make a different choice. He handed it to the police, a decision that tied him to Donovan Cross and set him on a path he could no longer stray from.

Since then, his career had soared, but at the cost of his soul. Every time he saw Evelyn's name, dragged through the mud in the papers—papers he now controlled—he felt a stab of guilt. But guilt was a luxury he could no longer afford. Guilt had become James' constant companion.

The phone on his desk buzzed, the screen displaying an unlisted number. James hesitated before answering, knowing who it would be. Donovan Cross's voice came through, cold and commanding, a constant reminder of the power he wielded.

"James, I assume you've seen the reports?" Cross's voice had the authority of someone who knew they were in control.

James swallowed hard. "Yes, we've been covering the arrests all day." The arrests were the top story, tied to an organized crime ring with suspected links to The Raven—a name that still sent shivers down his spine, though it had been years since he'd last heard it mentioned in connection with Horace.

"Good. Make sure it stays that way. We need to ensure the narrative remains clear—this is about law and order. No speculation, no digging into the past. Understood?"

"Understood," James replied, though the words felt heavy in his mouth. It was always the same with Cross—control the narrative, bury the truth.

"And James," Cross added, his tone lowering, "we can't afford any mistakes. Not now."

The line went dead, leaving James in the silence of his office, the weight of his choices pressing down on him. He had once believed in the power of the press to uncover the truth, to hold the powerful accountable. But now, he was part of the machinery that kept those truths hidden, all in the name of stability and control.

As he looked out over the city, his mind drifted back to the days when he had worked with Evelyn, back when they had been on the same side, driven by the same ideals. He wondered what she would think of him now, if she even thought of him at all.

A new message buzzed on his phone, this time with directives from Cross—more details on how to slant the coverage, to make sure certain facts were buried beneath the headlines. James read the message and felt the familiar pang of guilt, but he knew he would comply. He always did.

But something was different this time. As he placed the phone back on his desk, a memory surfaced, unbidden—the night they broke the story about the Obsidian Order, how it felt to be on the edge of something that mattered, something that could change the world. It had been dangerous, but it had been worth it. Back then, the risks had seemed justified, the fear manageable.

Now, the fear was different. It was the fear of being trapped, of being a puppet in a game he no longer controlled. The fear that one day, the truth would come crashing down, and when it did, there would be no escape.

James sighed and rubbed his temples, the weight of his choices pressing down harder than ever. He had made his bed, and he had to lie in it. But as he looked out over the city, he couldn't shake the feeling that the past was catching up to him, that the shadows were closing in. And for the first time in a long while, he wondered if he still had the strength to fight back—or if it was already too late.

CHAPTER 8:
FRACTURED TRUTHS

Evelyn Reid sat in the quiet gloom of her flat, her mind buzzing as she sifted through the remnants of the investigation that had shattered her life. Her hands trembled slightly as she opened the old file she'd managed to salvage from the wreckage of her career. The first page confronted her with a name that had haunted her for years: Donovan Cross.

She leaned back, narrowing her eyes as she studied the name. Cross, the elusive puppet master who had always stayed one step ahead. She had never been able to nail him, no matter how hard she tried. Every lead had vanished into thin air, every piece of evidence buried beneath layers of deception. But that was then, and this was now.

Now, she had time—time to look at everything again with fresh eyes. The file contained everything she had on him, meticulously gathered over years of chasing shadows. She flipped through the pages slowly, methodically, looking for patterns she might have missed, clues that hadn't made sense at the time.

Her eyes caught on a small detail she hadn't noticed before—an inconsistency in the timeline of events leading to Horace's arrest. The surveillance report that had sealed his fate placed him at a secret meeting with Raven operatives, a critical piece of evidence that had been used to convict him. But something about the date didn't add up.

She cross-referenced the report with Horace's testimony, which had placed him across the city at the same time. How could he be in two places at once? The question nagged at her, pulling her deeper into the puzzle. She retrieved her old notes, tracing the sequence of events. The timeline had always felt rushed, but now it was clear—someone had tampered with it.

Evelyn reached for her laptop, fingers flying across the keys as she pulled up public records, old emails, anything that might provide more context. She zoomed in on the surveillance footage mentioned in the report, analysing the frames, pausing, rewinding. The image quality was poor, grainy at best, but something caught her eye—a timestamp in the corner, slightly out of alignment with the rest of the video. Subtle, but there. Whoever had doctored the footage had been sloppy.

She scribbled notes furiously, connecting dots that had once seemed unrelated. The report was falsified, no doubt about it. And if this was false, what else had been manipulated? Evelyn dug deeper, cross-referencing dates and names. The falsified report coincided with a key moment in her career—the arson attacks in Edinburgh's Old Town. She remembered those days vividly, chasing a lead that had gone cold. The attacks had been blamed on a local gang, but she had always suspected there was more to the story.

She pulled out her old notes from the arson investigation, flipping through them with the same precision she had once brought to every story. There, buried in her scribbles, was a name she hadn't thought of in years: Callum Fraser, a firefighter she had interviewed. His statement had seemed like a dead end at the time —a vague description of a man in a suit, watching the flames from a distance, unbothered by the chaos around him. She had dismissed it back then, but now it felt like a missing piece of the puzzle. Could that man have been Donovan Cross?

Evelyn's mind raced as she pulled up Callum's contact information. She hesitated for a moment before dialling his number, unsure if he'd even remember her. The phone rang once, twice, then a gruff voice answered.

"Fraser here."

"Callum, it's Evelyn Reid. I don't know if you remember me—"

"Evelyn Reid? The reporter?" There was a pause, then a dry chuckle. "I thought you'd disappeared off the face of the earth."

"Not quite," she replied, forcing a smile. "I need to ask you about that fire in Old Town—do you remember the man in the suit you mentioned?"

There was a pause on the other end, then a sigh. "Yeah, I remember. Didn't think much of it at the time, but now... I dunno. Something didn't sit right with me about that guy."

"What if I told you that man might be connected to something much bigger?" Evelyn asked, her pulse quickening. "Something involving Horace MacLeod and The Raven."

Callum was silent for a moment, then his voice hardened. "If you're serious about this, I'll help. But you better be sure, Evelyn. Last time you got involved in something like this, it didn't end well."

She winced at the reminder. "I'm sure," she said quietly. "I need your help."

They arranged to meet, and Evelyn hung up, her heart pounding. This was it—the connection she had been missing. The arson attacks were a distraction, a cover for something bigger, something Cross had orchestrated. And that falsified report? It was all part of the plan, diverting attention from the real operation.

But as she pieced together the implications, the memories of the institution crept in—cold, sterile walls, staff speaking in hushed tones, treating her like a fragile object. Nights spent doubting her sanity, wondering if she'd imagined everything. Yet even in those dark moments, she had clung to the truth. Cross was real, and he was out there, pulling the strings.

Now, back in her flat, surrounded by the evidence she had fought so hard to keep, Evelyn felt the old fire reignite. Cross had taken almost everything from her, but he hadn't taken her will to fight. She knew the risks—Cross had crushed her once, and he wouldn't hesitate to do it again. But this time, she was ready. She had nothing left to lose, and that made her dangerous.

Evelyn spread out her notes, diagrams, and evidence across the table, reviewing every detail with meticulous care. The connections were clear now. Cross had orchestrated the arson attacks to distract from a larger operation, and he had used the falsified report to frame Horace and throw everyone off the scent.

The implications were staggering. If she could prove this, she could clear Horace's name and expose The Raven. But it wouldn't be easy. Cross had allies in high places, and the closer she got to the truth, the more dangerous it became.

She leaned back in her chair, exhaustion pulling at her, but she couldn't stop now. Not when she was so close. She had been broken, yes, but not destroyed. The fire that had once driven her was burning again, and this time, she wouldn't let it go out.

Evelyn stood, grabbing her coat and a recorder from her desk. She had work to do. The world had written her off as a flake, but they didn't know the fire that still burned within her. This time, she would follow the lead wherever it took her, and she wouldn't stop until the truth was out.

CHAPTER 9: DROWNING IN SHADOWS

Aidan stood in front of the bathroom mirror, his freshly cut hair framing a face he barely recognized. For the first time in what felt like years, he saw a man who looked like he was trying. The wild, unkempt look was gone, replaced by something cleaner, sharper. But as he stared at his reflection, doubts began to creep in, like shadows crawling over the edges of his resolve.

The silence in the apartment was heavy, pressing in on him from all sides. The sound of his own breathing filled the room, the only noise in the oppressive stillness. He reached up, touching the back of his head where the scissors had done their work. It should have felt like a victory—a small one, maybe, but a victory nonetheless. Yet, the satisfaction he had expected was fleeting, slipping away like sand through his fingers.

"Is this really who you are now?" he whispered to himself, his voice barely audible. "Or are you just pretending?"

The question hung in the air, unanswered. Aidan turned away from the mirror, moving back into the living room. The bottle of whiskey on the counter caught his eye, the same bottle he had ignored earlier in his burst of determination. It sat there, a silent challenge, daring him to make a choice.

His phone buzzed on the table, interrupting his thoughts. Aidan glanced at the screen—a message from an old contact, someone who still believed in him. The offer was tempting, the chance to dive back into the digital underworld, to feel that rush again. For a moment, he considered it. Maybe this was the way out. Maybe he could still be useful, still be someone.

But then he remembered why he had stopped. The thrill of the hack, the adrenaline of outsmarting the system—it had all come at a cost. Sophie's face flashed before his eyes, the disappointment in her eyes when she realized who he really was. Clarice's tiny hand, clinging to him for safety when he couldn't even protect himself.

Aidan sat down heavily on the couch, the weight of his thoughts pressing down on him. He knew what he wanted—he wanted to be better. But wanting and doing were two different things, and the gap between them felt impossibly wide.

The phone buzzed again. He picked it up, reading the message one more time. The temptation was there, stronger than ever. But so was the fear—the fear of losing everything he had tried to reclaim, of slipping back into the man he used to be.

"Not today," he muttered, tossing the phone aside. He stood up, pacing the length of the room, his thoughts a whirlwind of uncertainty. "Not today."

The bottle remained on the counter, untouched. Aidan walked past it, forcing himself to focus on anything else—on the small victories, on the fact that he had made it this far. He wasn't finished yet. There was still a long way to go, and the road would be rough. But for now, he had taken a step in the right direction.

CHAPTER 10: THE GILDED CAGE

Edinburgh bathed in the twilight, the wind tugged at the edges of Sophie's silk robe, but she barely noticed, her mind a tangled web of conflicting thoughts and emotions. The life she had built—the wealth, the comfort, the security—should have brought her peace. Instead, it had become a prison of her own making, with walls gilded in gold but cold to the touch.

As Sophie turned to go back inside, she heard a soft sound from Clarice's room. Instinctively, she moved toward the hallway, but when she reached the door, her heart stopped. The room was empty—Clarice's bed, once warm with her presence, was cold and undisturbed.

Panic gripped Sophie. She called out for Clarice, her voice trembling, but there was no answer. She searched every corner of the penthouse, her fear mounting with each passing second. It was as if Clarice had vanished into thin air.

Sophie's mind raced. The Raven. The thought struck her like a bolt of lightning. She had always known that her life of luxury came with strings attached, but this—this was a warning, a reminder that they controlled everything, even her daughter.

Just as she was about to call Donovan, the doorbell rang. Sophie rushed to the door, her heart pounding in her chest. She flung it open to find Mrs. Henderson, her elderly neighbour, standing there with Clarice in her arms. Relief washed over Sophie as she reached for her daughter, but the look in Mrs. Henderson's eyes stopped her cold.

"Found her wandering the hall," Mrs. Henderson said, her voice laced with something darker than concern. "Strange, isn't it? In a place like this, where the doors should be locked tight?"

Sophie froze, her breath catching in her throat. Mrs. Henderson had always been friendly, even grandmotherly, but there was something off about her now—a coldness that sent a chill down Sophie's spine.

"I—I don't know how she got out," Sophie stammered, taking Clarice into her arms, holding her close. The child seemed unbothered, as if she had just been on a little adventure.

"Oh, don't worry," Mrs. Henderson said, her smile never reaching her eyes. "These things happen. Children wander off. But it's important to keep a close eye on them, isn't it? You never know what could happen."

The underlying threat in her words was unmistakable. Sophie's heart pounded in her chest as she realized the truth—Mrs. Henderson wasn't just a kindly old neighbour. She was one of them. The Raven had eyes everywhere, even in the people Sophie thought she could trust.

"Thank you," Sophie managed to say, her voice barely above a whisper.

Mrs. Henderson's smile widened, and she reached out to pat Clarice on the head. "You take care now, dear. And remember—we're always watching."

With that, she turned and left, leaving Sophie standing in the doorway, trembling with a mix of fear and fury. As she closed the door, Sophie held Clarice tightly, her mind reeling. This wasn't just a warning—it was a declaration. The Raven owned her, and they weren't afraid to remind her of it.

She placed Clarice on the couch and sat beside her, trying to calm her racing heart. As she did, memories of that fateful day when she brought Clarice home from the hospital flooded her mind, unbidden and painful.

She remembered the joy she had felt holding Clarice for the first time. Despite the exhaustion, despite the fears, there had been a moment of pure, unadulterated happiness. But that happiness had been short-lived. The memory of Aidan, his breath tinged with alcohol as he took the driver's seat, surfaced like a dark cloud. Sophie had been too tired to argue, too overwhelmed by the birth and the prospect of bringing a newborn home. She had trusted Aidan, or perhaps she had just wanted to believe that he could handle it, that he was still the man she had once known.

The crash had been minor, barely more than a fender-bender, but in that split second, everything had changed. The jarring impact, the way Clarice had cried out in the back seat, the terror that had gripped Sophie as she realized how close they had come to something far worse. And then there was Aidan, his shame, his helplessness, as the realization of what he had done sank in.

She had seen it in his eyes, the moment he decided he couldn't stay. The crash was the final straw in a series of disappointments and betrayals, the moment that drove Aidan to walk away from them, leaving Sophie alone with a newborn and a life that was crumbling around her.

Sophie shook her head, trying to dispel the memory. It wasn't Aidan's fault, not entirely. They had both made mistakes, and they had both paid the price. But now, the price was being paid by Clarice, too, and that was something Sophie couldn't bear.

She put Clarice to bed, her hands still shaking. She watched her daughter sleep, the peaceful rise and fall of her chest a stark contrast to the turmoil raging inside her. The life she had chosen for them was supposed to be safe, secure. But now, it was clear—there was no safety, not even in their own home.

She moved back into the living room, her eyes falling on the small, ornate box on the mantel. Inside was the gun Donovan had given her, a symbol of her entrapment. She opened the box and stared at the cold metal, her anger growing with each passing second. The Raven might control her, but they didn't own her spirit. And if they thought they could use her daughter to keep her in line, they were wrong.

Sophie closed the box with a decisive snap and stood up, a new resolve hardening within her. She wouldn't be a pawn in their game any longer. For too long, she had let fear dictate her actions, but not anymore. There had to be a way to fight back, to protect Clarice from the darkness that surrounded them.

She didn't know how yet, but one thing was certain—Sophie would find a way to break free from The Raven's grasp. And when she did, they would regret ever thinking they could control her and threaten her baby girl.

CHAPTER 11: SHADOWS IN THE MIRROR

James Dyer sat at his desk, staring blankly at the flickering screen of his computer. The office around him was quiet, the hum of fluorescent lights the only sound breaking the silence. Despite the trappings of success—his corner office, the prestigious news channel he controlled—James felt trapped in a prison of his own making, one built of lies, betrayal, and fear.

The polished wood of his desk gleamed in the harsh light, a symbol of everything he had once worked for. But now, it felt like a cruel joke. Success, power, influence—none of it mattered anymore. Not when the cost had been so high. Not when he had traded his soul to Donovan Cross.

James rubbed his temples, trying to stave off the growing headache that had been plaguing him all day. But it wasn't the stress of the job causing it. It was the guilt—the crushing weight of the choices he had made and the people he had betrayed. The faces of those he had wronged haunted him, none more so than Evelyn Reid.

He had once respected Evelyn, even admired her tenacity and journalistic integrity. She had been a beacon of truth in a world full of deception. But all of that had changed the day Donovan Cross came into his life. It had started innocently enough—just a few favours, a little information passed along, nothing too serious. But Donovan had a way of tightening his grip, of making it clear that James's cooperation wasn't just appreciated; it was expected. And James had been too weak, too cowardly to resist.

The image of Evelyn's face flashed in his mind—her eyes wide with shock and betrayal the day he had handed her over to The Raven. He could still hear her voice, laced with disbelief, as she realized what he had done. The memory gnawed at him, an open wound that refused to heal.

James's phone buzzed, pulling him from his thoughts. He glanced down at the screen, his heart sinking as he saw the name: Donovan Cross.

With a shaky hand, he picked up the phone and read the message: "Need to talk. Now."

James swallowed hard, his mouth suddenly dry. He knew what this meant. Donovan was going to ask him for something, something that would push him even further down the path of no return. He considered ignoring the message, but the thought was fleeting. He knew Donovan wouldn't tolerate disobedience.

As he sat there, phone in hand, a memory surfaced—one he had tried to bury deep within his mind. It was the day his world had truly begun to unravel, the day The Raven had taken control of his life.

It had been a normal day, or so it seemed. James was wrapping up a broadcast when his phone rang. He recognized the number immediately—his younger brother, Luke. James and Luke had always been close, despite the ten-year age gap. Luke was still in university, full of life and potential, the one bright spot in James's increasingly dark world.

But when James answered the call, it wasn't Luke's voice on the other end. It was a voice he didn't recognize—cold, menacing.

"James Dyer?" the voice had asked, sending a chill down his spine.

"Who is this?" James had demanded, but deep down, he already knew something was terribly wrong.

"We have your brother," the voice replied, cutting through his fear like a knife. "He's safe, for now. But that depends entirely on you."

James's blood had run cold. He had tried to ask where Luke was, what they wanted, but the voice had been unyielding, refusing to answer his questions. Instead, they had told him what he needed to do—betray Evelyn Reid, feed her to The Raven, or Luke would suffer the consequences.

"You'll do as we say," the voice had said, each word dripping with malice. "Or your brother's blood will be on your hands."

The line had gone dead, leaving James in a state of shock. His first instinct had been to call the police, but even as he reached for the phone, he knew it was useless. The Raven had eyes everywhere, and they would know if he tried to involve the authorities. The terror he had felt in that moment was unlike anything he had ever experienced. The thought of losing Luke, of being responsible for his death, had been unbearable.

That night, James had sat in his office, staring at the photo of him and Luke on his desk, trying to figure out what to do. He had spent hours agonizing over the decision, but in the end, he had seen no other choice. He had betrayed Evelyn, handed her over to Donovan, and sealed her fate—all to save his brother.

But the guilt hadn't stopped there. Even after he had done what they asked, The Raven hadn't released Luke. They had kept him just out of reach, using him as leverage to ensure James's continued cooperation. Every time James thought he might break free, they would remind him of what was at stake—Luke's life, hanging in the balance.

Now, as he stared at the message from Donovan, the weight of that guilt bore down on him like a crushing wave. He was trapped, just as surely as Luke was, and there seemed to be no way out.

With a deep breath, James dialled Donovan's number. The phone barely rang once before Donovan answered, his voice as smooth and cold as ever.

"James," Donovan said, his tone laced with an underlying threat. "I trust you've been keeping an eye on things."

"Yes," James replied, trying to keep his voice steady. "Everything is under control."

"Good. I need you to make sure it stays that way. There's some information I need buried. You'll handle it."

James felt the familiar pang of guilt gnawing at him. Burying information, manipulating the truth—these were things he had once sworn he would never do. But now, it was just part of his daily routine.

"Of course," James said, the words tasting like ash in his mouth.

There was a pause on the other end of the line, and for a moment,

James thought Donovan might actually thank him. But instead, Donovan's voice took on a darker tone.

"And James," he added, "remember who put you where you are. Remember who you owe."

James nodded, even though Donovan couldn't see him. "I remember."

"Good," Donovan replied, and with that, the line went dead.

James sat there for a moment, the silence of the office pressing in around him. He had sold his soul to Donovan Cross, and every day he paid the price. The guilt was eating him alive, but he didn't see any way out. Donovan had him trapped, just like he had trapped so many others.

He turned back to his computer, his reflection faintly visible in the dark screen. It was a face he barely recognized anymore—a face marked by fear, regret, and self-loathing. He had betrayed Evelyn, sold her out to Donovan, and for what? A career? Power? None of it seemed worth it anymore.

The door to his office opened suddenly, and James flinched, his nerves on edge. It was just one of his assistants, bringing him some documents to sign. But the look of pity in her eyes, the way she quickly averted her gaze, told him everything he needed to know. Everyone could see what he had become.

As the door closed behind her, James let out a long, shaky breath. He was living a lie, and every day the walls of that lie were closing in on him. He could feel it—his time was running out. Sooner or later, Donovan would push him too far, ask for something James couldn't give. And when that happened, James knew there would be no escaping the consequences.

But for now, all he could do was keep playing the game, keep pretending that everything was fine. Because as long as Donovan held the strings, James knew he was nothing more than a puppet in his hands.

CHAPTER 12: WHISPERS IN THE DARK

Horace MacLeod sat on the edge of his prison cot, his fingers absently tracing the worn lines of the concrete wall beside him. The small cell was a far cry from the life he had once known, a life filled with purpose, respect, and the pursuit of justice. Now, all that remained were these four walls, closing in on him day by day, pressing the weight of his wrongful conviction onto his shoulders.

It had been months since the trial that had destroyed his career and condemned him to this place. The evidence had been overwhelming, fabricated with such precision that even Horace, in all his years of police work, hadn't seen it coming until it was too late. Donovan Cross had been the mastermind, of that Horace had no doubt, but proving it was another matter entirely. Here, in this cell, he was just another prisoner, a man whose life had been stolen by lies and deceit.

But there was one thing they hadn't taken from him—hope. It was faint, fragile, but it was there, flickering like a candle in the dark. Hope that one day, the truth would come to light, that the scales would be balanced, and that Donovan Cross would pay for his crimes. Horace clung to that hope, even as the days dragged on, each one blurring into the next.

He was lost in these thoughts when the guard came by during the evening round. Usually, the guards had little to say to him—most of them viewed him with a mix of disdain and pity, the once-great detective reduced to nothing. But tonight was different. The guard paused outside his cell, casting a quick glance down the corridor before slipping something through the bars.

Horace frowned, picking up the small slip of paper. The guard gave him a brief, unreadable look before moving on, leaving Horace alone with the mysterious note. His heart raced as he unfolded it, his eyes scanning the words written in a hurried, almost desperate script:

"Not all is lost. Keep fighting. There are those who still believe in you."

Horace stared at the note, his mind racing. Who could have sent this? Was it a trap, another cruel game orchestrated by Donovan to crush what little spirit he had left? Or was it genuine—an olive branch from someone who knew the truth, someone who might be able to help him?

He read the note again, searching for any clues, any hidden meaning, but it was too vague to decipher. Still, the message had an effect on him. For the first time in weeks, Horace felt a spark of something he had almost forgotten—determination. If there were people out there who believed in him, who knew the truth, then perhaps he wasn't as alone as he had thought.

Later that night, as the prison descended into its usual eerie quiet, Horace lay on his cot, his thoughts still circling around the note. The silence was suddenly broken by the sound of heavy footsteps outside his cell. Horace tensed, his instincts kicking in. Something was wrong.

The footsteps stopped, and for a moment, everything was still. Then, without warning, the cell door creaked open. Horace barely had time to react before two large figures burst into the cell, their faces obscured by the dim light. Before he could defend himself, they were on him, fists flying, blows landing with brutal efficiency.

Horace fought back, years of training and survival instincts driving him. He managed to land a few hits, but the men were strong, coordinated, and relentless. One of them pulled out a shiv, the sharp glint of the blade catching the faint light. Horace felt a sharp, searing pain as the blade found its mark, slicing through his side. He gasped, blood pouring from the wound, but he refused to go down easily.

Desperation fuelled him as he grabbed a loose brick from the wall, swinging it with all his might. It connected with one of the attackers' heads, sending him staggering back. But the second man was already on him, the shiv raised for another strike.

Just as the blade was about to come down, there was a shout from outside the cell. The attackers hesitated, their heads snapping toward the door. The moment of distraction was all Horace needed. He surged forward, slamming into the man with the shiv and knocking him to the ground. The other attacker, regaining his composure, lunged at Horace, but the sound of approaching guards made him think twice.

"Let's go!" one of them hissed, and within seconds, both men fled the cell, disappearing into the shadows as quickly as they had appeared.

Horace slumped against the wall, his hand pressed against the wound in his side. He was bleeding heavily, the pain nearly overwhelming, but he forced himself to stay conscious. The guards arrived moments later, shouting and demanding answers, but Horace's mind was already drifting, the world around him fading into a haze of pain and exhaustion.

As he was lifted onto a stretcher, the last thing he saw before everything went black was the slip of paper lying on the floor, a small reminder that somewhere out there, someone still believed in him.

CHAPTER 13: ECHOES OF BETRAYAL

The night was cold, the kind of cold that seeped into the bones and refused to let go. Donovan Cross stood in the shadows of a narrow alley, the city's lights casting long, eerie shapes across the cobblestones. He had always preferred the cover of darkness; it was where he did his best work, where he could manipulate the threads of power without interruption.

Tonight, though, something felt different. As he waited for his contact, his thoughts wandered back to the events that had set all of this in motion. The betrayal of Evelyn, orchestrated with precision; the calculated destruction of Horace's career; the slow, insidious corruption of James. Each step had been necessary, each move a part of a grander scheme to consolidate his control over Edinburgh.

But there was a part of him that could not forget the look in James's eyes when he had first been informed of Luke's abduction. It had been a brilliant stroke, ensuring James's loyalty through fear. Yet, as effective as it was, Donovan knew it was also a ticking time bomb. James's guilt was palpable, and guilt was a dangerous thing—it made people unpredictable.

His musings were interrupted by the arrival of his contact—a figure wrapped in a long coat, face obscured by the shadows. The contact handed Donovan a small package, their movements quick and efficient.

"The reports?" Donovan asked, his voice low.

"All here," the contact replied, their tone equally hushed. "They've started to move, just as you predicted. But there's something else... something we didn't anticipate."

Donovan's eyes narrowed. "What is it?"

"Horace... he survived the attack. Not only that, but he's started to gain the sympathy of some of the guards. There's talk among the inmates. If he continues to rally support..."

Donovan clenched his jaw. The attack on Horace had been meant to silence him permanently, to ensure that any lingering hope of exoneration was crushed. But it seemed that Horace was more resilient than he had anticipated.

"We'll need to apply more pressure," Donovan said, his voice like ice. "Make sure the guards know where their loyalties lie. And if Horace continues to be a problem... we'll deal with him another way."

The contact nodded and disappeared back into the shadows, leaving Donovan alone with his thoughts. The situation was more volatile than he liked, but he thrived in such conditions. Chaos was an opportunity, a chance to reassert control.

As Donovan moved through the alley and back towards his car, his mind returned to the trio—Horace, Evelyn, and Aidan. They were fractured, broken, but still dangerous in their own ways. And then there was Sophie, a wildcard in this deadly game. Her recent actions indicated a shift, a potential for rebellion that Donovan would have to crush before it gained momentum.

He couldn't afford any loose ends. The Raven's power was built on fear and control, and anything that threatened that control had to be eliminated.

Just as he reached the end of the alley, Donovan heard a noise— a soft gasp, followed by the scuffle of feet on the cobblestones. He turned, his eyes narrowing as he caught sight of a figure half-hidden behind a stack of crates. The figure—a young man, no more than a teenager—stared at Donovan with wide, terrified eyes.

"Who are you?" Donovan's voice was calm, almost bored, as he slowly approached the boy.

"N-no one," the boy stammered, backing away. "I didn't see anything, I swear..."

Donovan's lips curled into a cold smile. "It's too late for that, I'm afraid."

Before the boy could react, Donovan closed the distance between them, his movements swift and precise. The knife he pulled from his coat was a flash of silver in the dim light, and with a single, practiced motion, he drove it into the boy's side. The boy let out a choked gasp, his hands grasping at Donovan's coat as he sank to the ground.

Donovan knelt beside him, wiping the blade clean on the boy's shirt as life slowly drained from his eyes. There was no remorse in Donovan's expression, no hesitation in his actions. This was just another task, another loose end that needed tying up.

As the boy's body went limp, Donovan stood, casually straightening his coat. He glanced around the alley, ensuring that no one else had witnessed the scene. Satisfied, he calmly walked back to his car, the cold night air biting at his skin. There was no fear in Donovan, no concern that this act would come back to haunt him. He had done this countless times before, and he knew how to cover his tracks.

As he slid into the driver's seat, Donovan allowed himself a moment of reflection. This was the nature of power—the ability to snuff out lives without a second thought, to control the narrative and ensure that nothing and no one could threaten his dominion over Edinburgh.

He started the engine and drove off into the night, leaving the boy's body in the alley, another nameless victim of his ruthless ambition. Donovan was complacent, confident in his unassailable position. He had no fear of retribution, no doubt that he could continue to manipulate, control, and eliminate any threats to his reign.

But as the city lights flickered in his rearview mirror, a small, unnoticed crack had begun to form in the seemingly impenetrable facade of his empire. Donovan didn't see it, not yet—but the seeds of his downfall had been sown, and they were quietly, steadily growing.

CHAPTER 14: DAGGER OF THE MIND

Evelyn sat at her cluttered desk, the mess around her mirroring the turmoil in her mind. Papers, notes, and photographs were strewn across the surface, a chaotic web of her thoughts and investigations. The room felt suffocating, the air heavy with the weight of unfinished work and unanswered questions. She rubbed her temples, trying to stave off the familiar haze that had clouded her mind lately. The knock on the door startled her, snapping her out of her daze. Visitors were rare, and unexpected ones usually brought trouble.

She hesitated before standing, her fingers brushing against the cold metal of the revolver tucked into her desk drawer. "Who is it?" she called out, her voice tighter than she intended.

"It's Dr. Fisher. May I come in?"

Evelyn frowned. Dr. Caroline Fisher, her psychiatrist from the institution. What was she doing here? House calls weren't part of their arrangement, not since Evelyn had left the facility. Yet, something—whether curiosity or a deeper instinct—compelled her to open the door.

Dr. Fisher stood in the doorway, as polished and composed as ever. Her tailored coat and professional demeanour clashed with the disorder of Evelyn's flat. Her smile was warm, almost too warm, and Evelyn felt a familiar unease settling in the pit of her stomach. There was always something off about these visits, a sense of manipulation lurking beneath the surface.

"Evelyn," Dr. Fisher greeted her, stepping inside without waiting for an invitation. "I was in the area and thought I'd check in on you. How have you been?"

Evelyn closed the door behind her, masking her apprehension with a polite smile. "I've been managing. Trying to get back to some sort of normal."

Dr. Fisher nodded, her gaze sweeping across the room, lingering on the chaotic sprawl of notes and photographs. "It's good to see you keeping busy. Staying occupied is important for your recovery."

"Yeah, it helps," Evelyn replied cautiously, her tone guarded.

Dr. Fisher's eyes settled on Evelyn, her expression softening in that practiced way that always made Evelyn feel like she was being observed, analysed. "You know, I'm not here by coincidence. Your GP contacted me. They're concerned about you—mentioned you missed a couple of appointments and haven't been refilling your prescriptions as regularly as you should."

Evelyn's posture stiffened. She hadn't expected her GP to reach out to Dr. Fisher. "I've been busy," she said, her voice sharper than she intended. "But I'm still taking my medication."

"Good," Dr. Fisher said with a nod of approval, though her eyes betrayed a glint of something else. "But it's crucial to stay on top of it, Evelyn. You've made progress, but the road to recovery is a long one. I'm here to support you, even outside the institution."

Evelyn studied her, searching for any sign of hidden motives beneath the professional facade. Dr. Fisher's calm demeanour was unsettling, her concern almost too polished, too rehearsed. What was she really after?

After a few more moments of small talk, Dr. Fisher glanced at her watch and offered a practiced smile. "I should be going," she said. "But remember, if you need anything—anything at all—don't hesitate to call."

Evelyn nodded, following her to the door. "Thank you, Dr. Fisher. I appreciate it."

Dr. Fisher stepped out, and Evelyn turned to close the door. But in her preoccupied state, she didn't notice that the latch didn't catch. The door remained slightly ajar, a crack that Dr. Fisher quietly exploited. As Evelyn returned to her desk, her mind already drifting back to the tangle of thoughts waiting for her, she didn't hear the soft footsteps behind her.

Dr. Fisher waited in the hallway, listening intently until she was certain Evelyn was absorbed in her work. Then, with practiced stealth, she slipped back into the flat, the door closing silently behind her.

She moved through the apartment with quiet efficiency, making her way to the small bathroom off the hallway. The medicine cabinet creaked softly as she opened it, revealing the rows of prescription bottles inside. Dr. Fisher's eyes flicked over the labels, finding the one she was looking for. Evelyn's latest prescription.

With the precision of someone who had done this before, Dr. Fisher pulled out a small vial from her coat pocket. She carefully emptied several unmarked capsules into Evelyn's bottle, shaking it gently to mix them in. The drugs she added were stronger, more potent—designed to cloud Evelyn's mind further, to deepen her dependency.

Her task complete, Dr. Fisher paused for a moment, listening for any sign that Evelyn had noticed her presence. But the only sound came from the other room, the faint rustle of papers. Satisfied, she closed the cabinet, adjusting everything back to its original state.

Before leaving, Dr. Fisher took one last look around the flat. Her face remained impassive, betraying none of the cold calculation behind her actions. She had been careful, methodical—just as she always was. No one would suspect a thing.

With one final glance toward Evelyn's desk, where the woman sat hunched over her work, oblivious to the danger she was in, Dr. Fisher slipped out of the flat, this time ensuring the door closed softly behind her.

As she walked away, her footsteps echoing in the quiet hallway, a small, satisfied smile played at the corners of her lips. Evelyn would continue down the path she had set for her, guided by the very medications meant to help her. And Dr. Fisher would be there, watching, controlling, every step of the way.

CHAPTER 15:
CROSSROADS OF
CONSCIENCE

James Dyer sat in his office, the city lights outside his window casting long, ominous shadows across the room. He hunched over his desk, his fingers trembling as he scrolled through the messages on his phone. Each text from Donovan Cross was like a noose tightening around his neck, a constant reminder of the life he had chosen and the one he had lost. Tonight, though, the guilt that had been gnawing at him for months felt like an unbearable weight.

The walls of his corner office, once symbols of success, now felt like the bars of a cage. His achievements, the prestigious news channel he controlled, all seemed meaningless in the face of the fear that stalked him day and night. The fear wasn't just about Evelyn or Aidan anymore. It was about Luke—his younger brother, who had been the one bright spot in James's life.

Luke had been missing for months, abducted by The Raven to ensure James's loyalty. Donovan had promised Luke's safety as long as James did what was asked of him. But Donovan's promises were as thin as smoke. Luke had become nothing more than a ghost, a pawn in a game James no longer wanted to play.

The room was too quiet, the only sound the faint hum of the building's heating system. James's phone buzzed again on the desk, and he flinched, dread pooling in his stomach. He didn't need to check the screen to know who it was. Donovan Cross. The name alone sent a shiver down his spine.

With a deep breath, James picked up the phone, his hands shaking. The message was brief and cold, like every other communication from Donovan: "Time to deliver. Meet me at the usual place."

James stared at the words, his heart pounding in his chest. He knew what this meeting could mean—either he would continue down this path of betrayal, or he would find a way to break free. But did he even have the strength to fight back? The thought of facing Donovan filled him with a terror he couldn't shake. Yet, the thought of continuing to live under his thumb was even worse.

With trembling hands, James grabbed his coat and left the office, his steps unsteady as he made his way to the parking garage. The drive to the meeting spot was a blur, his mind consumed by images of Luke—bound, beaten, broken. Every red light, every stop sign felt like a countdown to his doom.

The meeting spot was an old warehouse on the outskirts of the city, one of Donovan's many hidden lairs. As James pulled up, the cold night air bit at his skin, a stark contrast to the heat of his anxiety. The warehouse loomed before him, dark and foreboding. He hesitated for a moment, his hand gripping the steering wheel so tightly his knuckles turned white.

But he couldn't turn back now. He couldn't leave Luke to suffer for his cowardice.

Inside, the warehouse was as cold and empty as his heart. Donovan stood in the middle of the room, a figure wrapped in shadow. The air between them was thick with tension, and James could feel his pulse hammering in his ears.

"You're late," Donovan said, his voice like ice.

James swallowed hard. "I'm here, aren't I?"

Donovan's gaze bore into him, unblinking, calculating. "I've been hearing things, James. Rumours that you've been... conflicted. That's dangerous—for both of us."

James felt the knot in his stomach tighten. This was it—the moment he had been dreading. He opened his mouth to speak, but Donovan cut him off with a sharp gesture.

"I need you to take care of something for me," Donovan continued, his tone deadly calm. "A message needs to be sent, and you're going to deliver it."

James's heart sank. He had done a lot of terrible things for Donovan, but this felt different. It felt final.

"What about Luke?" James asked, his voice barely more than a whisper. "You said he'd be safe."

A slow, cruel smile spread across Donovan's face. "Luke is safe, for now. But safety is a relative term, isn't it? It all depends on your actions."

James's blood ran cold. He could hear the unspoken threat in Donovan's words. Luke's life was hanging by a thread, and that thread was controlled by Donovan.

The realization hit James like a freight train. He had lost everything—his integrity, his friendships, his peace of mind—and for what? To keep his brother alive in a world where he was nothing more than a prisoner? The weight of his guilt was suffocating, and in that moment, something inside him snapped.

"I'm done, Donovan," James said, his voice trembling with fear and resolve. "I'm not doing this anymore."

Donovan's expression darkened, his eyes narrowing to slits. "You don't get to decide that, James. You're in this until I say you're out."

James shook his head, stepping back. "No. I'm not. Not anymore."

For a moment, the two men stared at each other, the tension crackling between them like electricity. Then, without warning, Donovan's hand shot out. The impact was brutal—a quick, decisive movement that sent James crashing to the ground.

He gasped for breath, the world spinning around him as he clutched his chest. The pain was intense, searing through him like fire. He could barely register Donovan's voice above him, cold and detached.

"You should have known better, James," Donovan said, his tone almost regretful. "There's no walking away from this."

Donovan wiped the blood from his blade and pocketed it, casting one last glance at James's crumpled form before turning on his heel and walking out of the warehouse. The sound of his footsteps echoed through the empty space, growing fainter with each step.

As the door slammed shut behind Donovan, the warehouse plunged into silence. James lay motionless on the cold concrete floor, his breaths shallow and ragged. The pain in his chest was excruciating, but as he slowly reached up to touch the wound, he felt something unexpected—the firm, unyielding material of the protective vest he had worn beneath his shirt. The blade had pierced the outer layer but hadn't reached his heart.

James's breath came in ragged gasps as he realized he was still alive. The vest had saved him, but Donovan didn't know that. To Donovan, James was dead—just another casualty in his ruthless quest for power.

James struggled to his feet, wincing with every movement. He had to be careful now. As far as Donovan was concerned, he was out of the picture, and that gave James a rare and dangerous opportunity. But he couldn't waste time—he needed to find Luke and get as far away from Donovan's reach as possible.

James stumbled out of the warehouse, he wondered if Donovan's complacence, his belief that he had removed another threat, could be the very thing that would lead to his downfall.

As James drove away into the night, his thoughts were consumed by a single, burning goal: to find his brother and bring down the man who had taken everything from him. Donovan Cross had made a fatal mistake, and James intended to make sure he paid for it.

CHAPTER 16:
THE BOTTOM OF
THE BOTTLE

Aidan Fraser couldn't remember the last time he'd felt anything other than numb. The days blurred together, one drink bleeding into the next, until all that remained was a dull ache in the pit of his stomach—a reminder of everything he'd lost, everything he'd thrown away.

It had been over a year since he'd walked away from Sophie and Clarice, convinced that they were better off without him. The memory of the crash still haunted him, replaying in his mind like a film he couldn't escape. Sophie's terrified eyes, Clarice's tiny cries —it was all he saw when he closed his eyes. It was all he heard in the silence that followed the chaos. He'd failed them in every way possible. Walking away had been easier than staying to face the consequences.

But easier didn't mean better.

Aidan's phone buzzed, pulling him from his thoughts. He ignored it at first, unwilling to engage with the world outside the haze of his self-imposed exile. But when the buzzing turned into a persistent chime, something made him reach for the phone, more out of irritation than anything else.

It was a notification from a social media app he hadn't bothered to delete. He hadn't looked at it in ages. Curiosity, or maybe something darker, compelled him to open it. The screen filled with an image of Clarice, smiling brightly in front of a birthday cake, candles flickering. "Happy 3rd birthday to my little angel!" the caption read. Sophie's words. Sophie's life, moving forward without him.

Aidan's chest tightened. Three years. He hadn't been there for any of it—her first steps, her first words, her first laugh. All of it had happened without him. He was nothing more than a ghost, a shadow that had faded from his daughter's life.

He scrolled through the photos, each one a knife twisting in his gut. Clarice surrounded by people he didn't know, people who had taken the place he should have filled. Her joy, her innocence —it was too much to bear. He had failed her, just as he had failed Sophie. The weight of that failure pressed down on him, suffocating, relentless.

The phone rang, jarring him out of his spiralling thoughts, but Aidan didn't reach for it. What could possibly be more important than the misery he was drowning in? But the ringing persisted, relentless and grating, until finally, with a growl of frustration, Aidan snatched the phone off the table.

"What?" he barked into the receiver, his voice rough from months of drinking.

"Aidan, it's James," came the voice on the other end. Tense. Urgent.

Aidan frowned, his mind still reeling from the images of Clarice. "James? What do you want?"

"There's no time to explain over the phone," James replied, his tone sharper than Aidan remembered. "I'm coming over. Don't do anything stupid until I get there."

Before Aidan could protest, the line went dead. He stared at the phone, confused and annoyed, but something in James's voice had cut through the alcohol-induced haze—a flicker of curiosity, maybe even concern.

When James arrived, Aidan could see it in his eyes—something was seriously wrong. His friend looked haggard, his posture tense, as if the weight of the world rested on his shoulders.

"What's going on?" Aidan asked, trying to push the images of

Clarice from his mind.

James didn't waste time. "Donovan tried to kill me," he said bluntly, his voice devoid of emotion. "He thinks I'm dead."

Aidan blinked, struggling to process the words. "Why would Donovan try to kill you?"

"Because I told him I was out," James replied, his voice steady but heavy with the weight of his confession. "I couldn't keep living with the guilt of betraying everyone I care about. And he tried to end me for it."

Aidan's mind raced, flashing back to the crash, the betrayal, the images of Clarice's birthday that still burned in his mind. Everything he'd been trying to bury was coming back to the surface, raw and unforgiving.

"I'm a mess, James," Aidan muttered. "I can't even take care of myself. How am I supposed to help you take down Donovan?"

James leaned forward, his eyes locking onto Aidan's with an intensity that cut through the fog. "You're wrong, Aidan. You're not a mess—you're a survivor. You've been through hell, and yet, you're still here. Right now, you're the only one who can help me. We need to find Luke, and we need to stop Donovan before he destroys anyone else."

Aidan shook his head, unable to meet James's gaze. "You don't know what I've become. I've lost everything that mattered."

James's voice softened, the tension easing slightly. "You think I don't know? Aidan, I've been there. We've both been lost— remember that night, before Sophie? The night we drank way too much and ended up... sharing more than just our secrets?"

Aidan froze, the memory flooding back. That night. They had both been in a dark place—James grappling with his own demons, and Aidan spiralling out of control. The alcohol had loosened their tongues, and before they knew it, they were sharing more than just their deepest fears. It had been a messy, drunken fumble, but it had also been a moment of vulnerability, a brief connection in a world that felt like it was falling apart.

James continued, his voice steady but laced with the weight of their shared past. "We were both lost, Aidan. We were both searching for something, anything to hold onto. And even though that night didn't mean what we thought it did, it showed me something about you. You're stronger than you know. You've faced the darkest parts of yourself and you're still standing. That's why I'm here, asking for your help."

Aidan looked up, meeting James's gaze. The vulnerability in his friend's eyes mirrored his own. They had both been through so much, and somehow, they had both survived. Maybe that meant something. Maybe it meant he wasn't as broken as he thought.

"I don't know if I can do this," Aidan whispered, his voice cracking. "I don't know if I'm strong enough."

James placed a hand on Aidan's shoulder, his grip firm. "You are, Aidan. You've always been strong, even when you didn't believe it. You're the one who taught me how to fight back, how to survive. Now I'm asking you to do it again. Not just for me, but for Sophie. For Clarice."

At the mention of his daughter's name, something inside Aidan shifted. The image of Clarice, the tiny, fragile life he had once held in his arms, filled his mind. He had walked away once, but maybe, just maybe, he could find a way back.

Aidan took a deep breath, the weight of his guilt and despair still pressing down on him, but for the first time in a long while, he felt a glimmer of resolve. He looked up at James, his eyes clear and determined.

"What do we do first?" Aidan asked, his voice steadier now.

James smiled, a small but genuine expression of relief. "First, we both get cleaned up. Then, we start planning."

As James helped Aidan to his feet, guiding him away from the remnants of his self-destruction, Aidan knew this was the beginning of a long, difficult road. But he also knew that for the first time in years, he had a purpose. He wasn't just fighting for himself anymore—he was fighting for Sophie, for Clarice, for

Horace and for the chance to make things right.
And this time, he wouldn't walk away.

CHAPTER 17: GATHERING THE PIECES

Evelyn Reid sat in her dimly lit basement flat, the soft glow of her computer screen reflecting off her tired eyes. Her desk was cluttered with papers, files, and photographs—evidence she had painstakingly gathered over the past year. The walls around her were covered in a chaotic array of newspaper clippings and notes, all connected by red string in a pattern only she could decipher. It was a tapestry of her thoughts, fears, and suspicions, all centred around one man: Donovan Cross.

The knock on her door was soft but insistent. Evelyn's heart skipped a beat. She wasn't expecting anyone, and unexpected visitors usually meant trouble. She reached for the small revolver she kept hidden in her desk drawer, just in case, before slowly making her way to the door.

"Who is it?" she called out, her voice steady despite the anxiety bubbling inside her.

"It's James."

The voice on the other side of the door made her pause. She hadn't heard from James Dyer in over a year, not since the last time he had refused to help her dig deeper into Donovan's affairs. But something in his tone made her put down the gun and open the door.

James stood there, looking more haggard and worn than she had ever seen him. His eyes were shadowed, his clothes dishevelled.

But there was a determination in his gaze that Evelyn hadn't seen before.

"Can I come in?" he asked quietly.

Evelyn stepped aside, allowing him to enter. As he walked past her, she noticed a slight tremor in his hands, a sign that something had shaken him to his core. She closed the door and turned to face him, crossing her arms as she studied him.

"What's going on, James? You look like you've seen a ghost."

James let out a hollow laugh as he sat down on the edge of her cluttered desk. "I might as well have. I'm lucky to be alive, Evelyn. Donovan tried to kill me."

Evelyn's breath caught in her throat. "What? Why?"

"Because I told him I was out," James said, his voice filled with a mixture of fear and anger. "I couldn't do it anymore. I couldn't live with the guilt of what I've done. So I tried to break free, and he tried to end me for it."

Evelyn shook her head in disbelief, her mind racing to catch up with what he was saying. "But you're here. How did you survive?"

"I was lucky. I was wearing a protective vest, but Donovan doesn't know that. As far as he's concerned, I'm dead."

The room fell silent as Evelyn processed this information. James being alive was a miracle, but it also meant that he was now in even more danger than before. And if Donovan found out he was still breathing, there would be no second chances.

"What are you going to do?" Evelyn asked, her voice barely above a whisper.

James looked up at her, his expression grim. "I'm going to bring him down. But I can't do it alone, Evelyn. I need your help."

Evelyn stared at him, her mind flashing back to all the times she had tried to get him to see the truth, to join her in her fight against Donovan. And now, after all this time, he was finally asking for her help.

"What changed, James? Why now?"

James sighed, running a hand through his hair. "Because I've done terrible things, Evelyn. Things I can't undo. Donovan's been holding my brother hostage, forcing me to do his bidding. I helped frame Horace, and I lied to everyone about it. But I can't keep living this lie. I have to make things right, for Horace, for my brother, and for everyone Donovan has hurt."

Evelyn froze, her heart pounding in her chest as the words sank in. "What did you just say?" she asked, her voice dangerously calm.

James looked up at her, his expression filled with guilt. "I'm the reason Horace is in prison. Donovan forced me to help frame him."

For a moment, the room was deathly silent. Then, like a dam breaking, a surge of fury washed over Evelyn. "You... you did this?" she spat, her voice trembling with rage. "You're the reason Horace has been rotting in that hellhole for the past three years?"

James flinched at the venom in her tone, but he didn't look away. "Yes, Evelyn. And I hate myself for it every single day. But I didn't have a choice. Donovan threatened to kill my brother. I had to do it to keep him alive."

Evelyn's hands clenched into fists, her whole body trembling with the intensity of her emotions. "Do you have any idea what you've done? Horace is innocent, and you let them lock him away like a common criminal! I've spent every waking moment trying to prove his innocence, and you... you knew all along!"

James nodded, his own voice shaking with guilt and regret. "I know, Evelyn. And I'll never forgive myself for it. But I'm trying to make things right now. I need your help to bring Donovan down, to clear Horace's name."

Evelyn glared at him, the anger and betrayal burning in her chest. She had trusted James, believed that he was a good man despite everything, and now she felt like a fool. "How dare you come here and ask for my help after everything you've done? You're no better than Donovan."

James recoiled as if she had slapped him, pain flashing in his eyes. "Maybe you're right," he said quietly. "Maybe I don't deserve your help. But I'm begging you, Evelyn. Not for me, but for Horace. He deserves to be free, and I can't do this without you."

Evelyn turned away, trying to control the storm of emotions raging inside her. She wanted to scream, to throw him out of her flat and out of her life forever. But then she thought of Horace, alone in that prison, suffering for a crime he didn't commit. And she knew that as much as she hated James right now, she couldn't walk away from this. Not if it meant getting justice for Horace.

Slowly, she turned back to face him, her eyes still blazing with anger. "I'm not doing this for you," she said coldly. "I'm doing this for Horace. But if you ever lie to me again, James, I swear I will make you regret it."

James nodded, the relief evident in his eyes despite the tension between them. "I understand. No more lies. No more secrets."

Evelyn took a deep breath, the weight of the past year lifting slightly. There was still so much to do, so much to fight for, but for the first time in a long while, she didn't feel so alone.

"Let's finish what we started," she said, her voice filled with resolve. "Let's bring Donovan down and clear Horace's name."

James nodded, his expression serious. "Together."

As they began to discuss their next steps, the tension between them still simmered, but there was a shared determination now. They both knew the stakes, and they both had a lot to atone for. But with their combined efforts, they stood a chance of finally bringing Donovan to justice and freeing Horace from the nightmare that had been his life for the past three years.

CHAPTER 18: THE TIES THAT BIND

Sophie Dawson stood at the window of her luxurious rooftop apartment, gazing out over the Edinburgh skyline. The city lights twinkled below her, but her mind was far from the glittering view. She had built a life of comfort and privilege, but it was a life built on compromise and darkness. The Raven had given her everything she needed to survive after Aidan left, but at a cost she was no longer willing to pay.

Her thoughts were interrupted by a soft knock on the door. Sophie's heart raced—visitors at this hour were rare, and she couldn't afford to be caught off guard. She moved cautiously toward the door, peering through the peephole to see who it was.

Her breath caught in her throat when she saw Aidan standing there, looking more sober and serious than she had seen him in years. She hesitated for a moment before opening the door, a mix of emotions surging through her—relief, anger, hope, and fear.

"Aidan," she said, her voice barely above a whisper.

"Sophie," Aidan replied, his voice thick with emotion. "I need to talk to you. About everything."

Sophie stepped aside, allowing him to enter. As he walked in, she noticed how much he had changed. His once wild and unkempt appearance had been replaced with a look of determination. He was still worn and weary, but there was a clarity in his eyes that hadn't been there before.

Aidan took a deep breath, gathering his thoughts before speaking. "I know I've been a mess. I know I've hurt you and Clarice, and I'm sorry. But I'm trying to make things right. I want to be the father Clarice deserves and the man you believed in."

Sophie felt a lump form in her throat. She had waited so long to hear these words, but now that they were finally being spoken, she didn't know how to respond. "Aidan... it's been so long. So much has happened."

"I know," Aidan said, stepping closer to her. "And I can't change the past. But I want to be here for you, for both of you. I need your help, Sophie. I can't do this alone."

Sophie looked into his eyes, searching for the sincerity she so desperately needed to see. And there it was—Aidan was truly trying to change, to atone for his mistakes. But there was still fear in her heart, fear of being hurt again.

"What is it that you need help with?" Sophie asked cautiously.

Aidan sighed, running a hand through his hair. "Donovan Cross. He's the reason everything fell apart. He's the one who manipulated us all, who framed Horace, who's been holding James's brother hostage. We're planning to bring him down, but I need you with me. We need to protect Clarice, and we need to stop him before he hurts anyone else."

Sophie's eyes widened at the mention of Donovan. She had always known there was more to The Raven's operations than what she was told, but she hadn't realized the full extent of Donovan's reach. The thought of going up against him terrified her, but the thought of not doing anything, of letting him continue to destroy lives, was even worse.

"What do you need me to do?" Sophie asked, her voice trembling slightly.

"Help me protect Clarice," Aidan said, his voice filled with urgency. "And help us gather evidence against Donovan. You know more about The Raven's operations than anyone. If we can expose him, we can take him down."

Sophie took a deep breath, her mind racing. She had never imagined she would be in this position, but as she looked at Aidan, she realized she couldn't walk away from this fight. She had to do what was right, for herself, for Clarice, and for the man she had once loved.

"Okay," Sophie said, her voice firm. "I'm in. But Aidan, if we're going to do this, you have to be all in. No more running away."

Aidan nodded, his expression serious. "I'm all in, Sophie. I promise."

They stood in silence for a moment, the weight of their decision hanging between them. Then, as if a silent agreement had been made, they embraced, finding comfort in each other's presence after so long apart.

Later that night, Aidan and Sophie met with James and Evelyn in a discreet location. The tension between them was palpable, but there was also a sense of shared purpose.

"Glad you could make it," James said, nodding to Sophie as she and Aidan entered.

Sophie returned the nod, still wary but determined. "We need to talk strategy. Donovan's not going to go down easily."

Evelyn, who had been quietly listening, finally spoke up. "I've gathered enough evidence to implicate Donovan, but we need more. We need something concrete that will tie him to the crimes we know he's committed."

"And we need to find Luke," James added. "He's the key to all of this. If we can get him out, he can testify against Donovan."

Aidan leaned forward, his mind already racing with possibilities. "What if we use the media against Donovan? James, you still have contacts at the news station, right? We could leak some of what we know, create a media storm that forces Donovan to make a mistake."

James considered this, nodding slowly. "It's risky, but it could work. If we expose just enough to make Donovan nervous, he might act rashly. But we need to be careful—if we reveal too much, he could go underground and disappear."

Sophie chimed in, her tone thoughtful. "We could use the information we already have to create a false narrative— something that looks like a scandal but isn't directly connected to us. If Donovan thinks the threat is coming from someone else, he might let his guard down."

Evelyn nodded, her mind already piecing together the plan. "And while he's distracted, we gather the real evidence. Aidan, you have the technical skills to hack into The Raven's systems, right? If we can access their internal communications, we might find something that directly links Donovan to the crimes."

Aidan's eyes lit up at the challenge. "I can do that. I'll need some time to set up a secure connection and bypass their firewalls, but it's doable. Once we're in, we can download everything we need."

"And if we time it right," James added, "we can drop the media bombshell and execute the hack simultaneously. That way, if Donovan tries to cover his tracks, we'll already have what we need."

Sophie looked around at the group, her heart pounding with a mixture of fear and excitement. "This could work. But we need to be careful—one wrong move, and we're all done for."

Evelyn nodded in agreement. "We'll need to stay coordinated, keep communication open, and make sure we're ready to move at a moment's notice."

James looked at each of them, his expression serious. "This is it. We either take Donovan down together, or we fall apart trying. But if we stick to the plan, we have a real chance of ending this nightmare."

The group exchanged determined looks, each of them understanding the gravity of the situation. The plan was risky, but it was their best shot at taking down Donovan once and for all.

As they finalized their strategy, there was a sense of urgency in the room. The stakes were higher than ever, and failure was not an option.

CHAPTER 19: REFORMATION

The night had settled over Edinburgh, casting a familiar chill through the narrow alleys and winding streets. The group gathered in an abandoned office space just off North Bridge, the heart of the city pulsating around them, yet they were cocooned in their own world of secrecy and tension. Their faces were lit by the glow of laptop screens, the muted hum of the city outside only adding to the intensity inside.

Aidan sat at the central terminal, his fingers flying across the keyboard as he bypassed The Raven's firewalls. His focus was razor-sharp, the familiar architecture of Edinburgh reflected in his thoughts as he visualized the route they'd need to take. James paced behind him, the weight of the night heavy on his shoulders.

"Got it," Aidan muttered, leaning back slightly, his eyes fixed on the screen. "I'm in. Accessing their communications now."

James stopped pacing, the tension in his body momentarily easing. "Good. Now let's find Luke."

Aidan glanced over his shoulder, a hint of a smirk playing on his lips. "You know, James, if you hadn't gotten mixed up with Donovan in the first place, we could've spent the night at the Royal Mile, having a drink instead of doing this. But I guess that would've been too easy, huh?"

James chuckled dryly. "Where's the fun in easy? Besides, this city's seen enough history—might as well add our names to the list of legends, right?"

"Legendary or infamous, not much of a difference," Sophie chimed in from her spot by the window, looking out towards Arthur's Seat, the silhouette of the hill looming like a silent sentinel over the city. "You've got a twisted sense of entertainment, Dyer."

"Hey, if we're going to face down a criminal mastermind, we might as well do it with some style," James replied with a wry grin.

Evelyn rolled her eyes, unable to suppress a smile. "I'd settle for getting through this without losing another piece of my sanity, thank you very much."

Aidan's focus returned to his screen. "Alright, I've found something. Looks like Donovan's keeping Luke in a secure facility near the docks—Leith, just off Ocean Drive. It's an old warehouse, refitted for their purposes. He's got guards on rotation, but they're not expecting anyone to come looking."

James nodded, a mix of relief and anxiety in his voice. "That's good. We've still got the element of surprise. But we need to move fast before Donovan realizes we're onto him."

Sophie leaned forward, her gaze sharp. "What's the plan, then? We can't just waltz down Leith Walk and expect them to hand Luke over."

Aidan shot her a sidelong glance. "Why not? I hear Donovan's guards are very reasonable guys. We'll just explain the situation, and they'll invite us in for tea."

Sophie snorted. "Sure, and then they'll shoot us in the back while we're sipping Earl Grey."

"Not if we outsmart them first," Aidan replied, a mischievous glint in his eye. "We'll create a distraction, something to draw their attention away from the main entrance. While they're busy chasing shadows near The Shore, we slip in through the back."

Evelyn nodded thoughtfully. "I can create a diversion. I've been tracking Donovan's media coverage, and I've got a few contacts near Waverley Station who owe me favours. A well-timed news story could send Donovan scrambling, giving us the window we need."

James looked at her with admiration. "You never cease to amaze me, Evelyn. Always ten steps ahead."

Evelyn gave him a small, almost shy smile. "Let's just say I've learned from the best."

Aidan leaned back, folding his arms. "So, we've got a plan. Now we just need to execute it. Sophie, you're with me on the tech front. We'll handle the security systems and make sure our path is clear. James, you and Evelyn get ready to extract Luke."

Sophie raised an eyebrow. "What, no witty comment about my hacking skills?"

Aidan grinned. "I figured I'd let your actions speak for themselves this time. But don't get used to it."

As the group finalized their plan, the camaraderie between them was evident. The banter, though light-hearted, was a testament to the underlying respect they had for one another. They were more than just allies in a fight against Donovan—they were a team again, bound together by the shared goal of taking down a man who had caused them all so much pain.

With the plan set, the group moved into position, each of them focused and ready for what was to come.

As Aidan and Sophie began their part of the operation, disabling security systems with precision and skill, James and Evelyn prepared for the extraction. The tension was palpable, but it was tempered by the confidence that they had each other's backs.

As they neared the warehouse in Leith where Luke was being held,

James couldn't help but glance at Evelyn, a hint of concern in his eyes. "You ready for this?"

Evelyn met his gaze, her expression resolute. "I've been ready since the day Donovan took everything from us."

James nodded, feeling a surge of determination. "Let's bring Luke home."

CHAPTER 20: BREAKING THE CHAINS

The darkness of Edinburgh's night was thick as the group moved silently through the narrow streets of Leith. The docks were quiet, save for the occasional distant hum of machinery and the soft lapping of the Firth of Forth against the shore. The old warehouse they approached was a relic from the past, its weathered bricks and rusted metal doors now serving a more sinister purpose under Donovan's command.

Aidan, Sophie, James, and Evelyn huddled together in the shadows just outside the warehouse perimeter. Aidan adjusted the small earpiece in his ear, his fingers tapping commands into his handheld device. The security cameras, which once stood as silent sentinels, now looped on a harmless feed, leaving the group undetected.

"This still doesn't erase what you did.", said Aiden.

Aidan found himself double-checking the intel James provided, his training overriding his heart.

"I didn't have a choice, Aidan.", James replied anxiously and muted.

"Maybe. But that doesn't make it any easier to swallow.", to Aiden it wasn't forgiveness, but it was a start. "Okay. Cameras are down," Aidan whispered, his voice barely audible. "We've got ten minutes before the backup system kicks in."

James nodded, his eyes scanning the area for any signs of movement. "That's all we need. Let's move."

The group split into two pairs, with Aidan and Sophie heading to the back entrance to disable the remaining security measures while James and Evelyn approached the front. The plan was simple: create a distraction, get Luke, and get out. But simplicity didn't make it any less dangerous.

As Aidan and Sophie crept towards the rear of the warehouse, the tension between them was palpable. They had worked together before, but never with so much at stake. The air was thick with the unspoken weight of their shared past, but there was no time to dwell on it now.

"Do you remember the first time we did something like this?" Sophie whispered, her voice laced with a hint of nostalgia.

Aidan smirked, keeping his eyes on the door. "Yeah. Back in those days, it was for fun—or at least, that's what we told ourselves."

Sophie nodded, her eyes scanning the darkness. "We were invincible back then. Or so we thought."

"Invincible," Aidan echoed with a touch of bitterness. "Funny how that changes when real lives are on the line."

Sophie glanced at him, her expression softening. "We're doing this for real this time, Aidan. For Luke, for us. We're not those kids anymore."

Aidan paused, looking at her for a moment longer than necessary. "No, we're not. But we're still in this together. Let's make it count."

Sophie gave him a small, determined smile before turning her attention back to the task at hand. With a few quick taps on the keypad beside the door, she deactivated the final security system. The door clicked open, revealing a dimly lit corridor inside.

Meanwhile, at the front of the warehouse, James and Evelyn prepared to make their move. Evelyn's contact had come through, and just as planned, a breaking news story began airing across every major channel in Edinburgh, exposing a fabricated scandal linked to Donovan. It was enough to cause a stir, pulling some of his men away from their posts to deal with the fallout.

James adjusted his jacket, feeling the weight of the gun concealed beneath it. He hadn't wanted to carry a weapon, but in the world they were operating in, it was a necessary evil. He glanced at Evelyn, her focus sharp, her resolve unshakable.

"You've got that look again," James said quietly, a hint of a smile playing on his lips.

"What look?" Evelyn asked, not breaking her concentration.

"The one that says you're about to take on the world and win."

Evelyn's lips twitched into a smile. "I've had plenty of practice."

James nodded, his expression turning serious. "Let's just make sure we both walk out of here."

Evelyn looked at him, her eyes softening for just a moment. "We will. We've come too far to fail now."

With a shared nod, they moved forward, slipping into the shadows as they approached the main entrance. The guards who were meant to be stationed there were distracted by the news on their phones, allowing James and Evelyn to slip past unnoticed.

Inside the warehouse, the atmosphere was tense, the air heavy with anticipation. The group converged in the main corridor, each of them on high alert as they made their way toward the room where Luke was being held. Aidan checked the layout on his device, pointing down a side passage.

"This way," he whispered, leading the group down the narrow hall.

The sound of their footsteps was barely a whisper on the concrete floor, but to them, it echoed like thunder. The door at the end of the hall loomed ahead, the only thing standing between them and Luke. Aidan moved to the front, reaching for the handle, his pulse pounding in his ears.

"Ready?" he asked, his voice steady despite the adrenaline surging through him.

"Do it," James replied, his voice tight with anticipation.

Aidan pushed the door open, revealing a small, dimly lit room. Luke was there, bound to a chair, his face bruised and battered but his eyes still defiant. At the sight of his brother, James felt a rush of relief and anger all at once.

"James," Luke croaked, his voice hoarse. "Took you long enough."

James rushed forward, pulling a knife from his pocket to cut the ropes binding Luke's wrists. "I'm sorry, Luke. I'm so sorry."

Luke shook his head, wincing as he tried to stand. "Don't be. You came. That's all that matters."

Sophie and Evelyn kept watch at the door while Aidan helped James support Luke, the urgency of the situation driving them forward. But just as they started to move, a loud crash echoed through the building, followed by the sound of approaching footsteps.

"They know we're here," Evelyn hissed, her grip tightening on her weapon.

"Time to go," Aidan said, his voice tense. "We stick to the plan. Sophie, get us out of here."

Sophie nodded, her fingers flying across the keypad of her device. "I've set a loop on the security feeds and triggered a fire alarm in the main building. That should buy us a few minutes."

The group moved quickly, supporting Luke as they made their way back through the corridors. The sound of the alarm blaring through the warehouse added to the chaos, but it also masked their movements, allowing them to slip past the guards who were now scrambling to respond to the alarm.

As they neared the exit, the situation grew more perilous. The guards were converging on their location, and it was only a matter of time before they were discovered. Aidan, ever the strategist, scanned the area for a way out, his mind racing.

"There!" he pointed to a side door leading to a back alley. "That'll take us to the waterfront. We can lose them in the docks."

With no time to argue, the group pushed forward, bursting through the door and into the cold night air. The docks stretched out before them, a maze of shipping containers and cargo ships, the perfect place to disappear.

But the sound of pursuing footsteps grew louder, and it was clear they were running out of time. As they raced towards the docks, Aidan glanced at Sophie, his voice low and urgent.

"Remember the time we outran the cops on Calton Hill?"

Sophie shot him a grin, despite the danger. "How could I forget? You nearly got us killed."

"Looks like we're about to do it again," Aidan replied, his eyes gleaming with adrenaline.

They reached the edge of the docks, the dark waters of the Firth of Forth lapping against the pier. With no time to think, they slipped between the rows of containers, using the shadows to their advantage.

But just as they thought they were in the clear, a spotlight suddenly cut through the darkness, pinning them in place. The guards had caught up, their weapons raised, ready to fire.

"Stay down!" James shouted, pulling Luke to the ground as the others followed suit.

The situation was dire, and they were out of options. But in that moment, Evelyn's voice cut through the tension, calm and controlled.

"Trust me," she whispered, her eyes fixed on the guards.

Before anyone could react, she stood up, raising her hands in a gesture of surrender. The guards hesitated, unsure of what to make of the situation.

"Don't shoot!" Evelyn called out, her voice steady. "We're unarmed!"

The guards approached cautiously, their weapons still trained on the group. But just as they reached Evelyn, she moved with lightning speed, disarming the nearest guard with a quick twist of her wrist. The others reacted, but the brief distraction was all Aidan and Sophie needed to spring into action, taking down the remaining guards with precise, practiced movements.

Within moments, the threat was neutralized, and the group was back on their feet, moving swiftly towards the safety of the waterfront. They reached a small boat moored at the pier, their escape route planned in advance.

As they helped Luke onto the boat, Aidan glanced back at the warehouse, the weight of what they had just done settling over him. They had succeeded, but they weren't out of the woods yet.

"Everyone on board," Aidan urged, his voice tight with urgency. "We need to get out of here before they send reinforcements."

The group piled onto the boat, the engine roaring to life as they sped away from the docks, the lights of Edinburgh fading into the distance.

As they sailed into the darkness, the city behind them, James sat beside his brother, his heart filled with both relief and fear. They had made it this far, but Donovan wouldn't let them go easily. As the boat cut through the dark waters, James looked at his companions, each of them battered but unbroken.

"Thank you," he said quietly, his voice filled with gratitude. "I couldn't have done this without you."

"We're not done yet," Aidan replied, his gaze fixed on the horizon. "Donovan will come after us. We need to be ready."

CHAPTER 21: ORCHESTRATED PAYBACK

The dawn light barely touched the horizon as the boat cut through the calm waters of the Firth of Forth. The tension from the night's escape still hung heavily over the group, but there was a palpable shift in their energy. They had succeeded in rescuing Luke, but they knew this was just the beginning of the end.

As they approached a secluded dock near Queensferry, Aidan steered the boat carefully to the shore. The area was remote, far from the prying eyes of the city, making it the perfect spot for a temporary refuge. The group disembarked in silence, each of them deep in thought, processing the events of the night.

Luke, though bruised and battered, was resolute as he stepped onto solid ground. He leaned on James for support, but there was a fire in his eyes that hadn't been there before.

"What now?" Sophie asked, her voice breaking the silence as they made their way up the narrow path leading from the dock.

James glanced at his brother, then at the rest of the group. "Now, we finish this."

Evelyn nodded, her gaze focused ahead. "We have everything we need to expose Donovan. The evidence, Luke's testimony—it's all enough to bring him down."

"But we need to do it smart," Aidan added, his mind already working through the logistics. "If Donovan gets even a whiff of what we're planning, he'll go underground, and we'll never find him again."

"We've already set things in motion," Evelyn said, pulling out her phone. "The media story I planted has spread like wildfire. The public is asking questions, and Donovan's under pressure to respond."

James's expression hardened. "Good. Let him squirm. But we need to be ready for his retaliation. He won't go down without a fight."

They reached a small cabin hidden among the trees, a temporary hideout they had prepared for just this moment. Inside, the cabin was simple but equipped with everything they needed—communication devices, supplies, and a sense of security.

As they settled in, Aidan and Sophie set up the equipment, ensuring they could monitor any communications from Donovan's network. Evelyn contacted her media allies, feeding them the final pieces of the puzzle to ensure the story would break wide open.

Luke, still recovering, sat by the window, watching the sun rise over the water. "I never thought I'd see daylight again," he murmured, more to himself than to anyone else.

James joined him, placing a hand on his brother's shoulder. "You're safe now, Luke. We'll make sure of that."

Luke looked at him, his eyes filled with determination. "I want to help. Donovan took everything from me. I'm not going to let him walk away from this."

James smiled grimly. "Neither are we."

As the morning unfolded, the group worked tirelessly to finalize their plan. Every detail was scrutinized, every potential risk considered. They knew they had one shot at this, and they couldn't afford any mistakes.

Aidan's skills were put to the test as he worked on setting up the most critical component of their operation: the transmission system. Using a series of encrypted servers, Aidan created a digital broadcast platform that would bypass traditional media channels, ensuring that their message would reach the widest audience possible without interference.

He had designed a multi-layered firewall system that would protect their data from being traced back to them. Every piece of information they were about to release would be distributed through a network of proxy servers scattered across the globe, making it nearly impossible for Donovan or his allies to shut it down.

Sophie, meanwhile, was in charge of the social media front. Using sophisticated bots and algorithms, she orchestrated a digital assault, ensuring that their message would trend across all platforms within minutes of its release. She set up fake accounts, seeded hashtags, and coordinated with Evelyn's media contacts to create a wave of public outrage that would be impossible to ignore.

"Everything is set," Aidan said, his fingers still moving across the keyboard. "Once we hit send, there's no going back. This will be out there for everyone to see."

Evelyn leaned over his shoulder, watching the screen. "Let's make sure it counts."

With the final touches in place, they prepared for the broadcast. Aidan had written a script that would be read by a synthesized voice, ensuring their anonymity while delivering the damning evidence. The message would be accompanied by video footage, documents, and testimonies—all irrefutable proof of Donovan's crimes.

The group gathered around the monitors, the weight of the

moment settling over them. This was it—the culmination of all their efforts, their pain, and their determination.

The Transmission

As the clock struck noon, Aidan hit the send button, and the transmission went live. Instantly, the digital wave spread across the internet. News sites, social media platforms, and independent blogs were flooded with the information they had released.

The broadcast was both concise and damning. The voice spoke with cold, calculated precision as it detailed Donovan's rise to power, his connections to organized crime, and his manipulation of the media and law enforcement. The evidence was displayed on the screen, undeniable and irrefutable.

Within minutes, the impact was felt. News anchors interrupted their regular programming to cover the breaking story, social media exploded with the hashtags Sophie had planted, and the public reaction was immediate and fierce.

The Impact

As the minutes ticked by, the group watched the chaos unfold in real-time. Aidan's systems tracked the spread of the information, monitoring the responses from media outlets, public figures, and law enforcement. The pressure was mounting on Donovan, and they could see it in the panicked communications coming from his network.

"He's trying to shut it down," Aidan said, his eyes scanning the data streams. "But it's too late. This is everywhere."

Evelyn smiled grimly. "Good. Let him try."

The broadcast had not only exposed Donovan but had also implicated several of his closest allies. Politicians, business leaders, and law enforcement officials were being named and shamed, their connections to The Raven laid bare for all to see.

As the fallout continued, Luke sat back, a sense of satisfaction washing over him. For the first time in years, he felt like justice might actually be within reach.

The Retaliation

But they knew Donovan wouldn't go down without a fight. Afterall the signal blocker Aidan had set up was only temporary and as expected, the retaliation came swiftly.

Aidan's phone buzzed with an incoming alert. He glanced at the screen, his expression darkening. "He's sending men after us. He's not going down quietly."

James tightened his grip on his weapon, his resolve hardening. "Let them come. We're ready."

Evelyn's eyes were sharp, her voice filled with quiet determination. "This ends today."

As they braced for the final showdown, the group knew they were on the brink of something monumental. The fall of Donovan Cross was within their grasp, but at what cost would this come?

The stage was set for the ultimate confrontation.

CHAPTER 22: BLOOD AT DAWN

The aftermath of the digital onslaught was swift and brutal. Within hours, Edinburgh was ablaze with the revelations, and Donovan's empire was crumbling under the weight of public outrage and legal scrutiny. The group, however, had no time to savour their victory as they prepared for what was likely to be Donovan's final, desperate move.

The Final Stand

As the sun began to set over the city, casting long shadows across the streets, Aidan monitored the incoming signals. His system, which had been used to spread the damning information, was now detecting increased chatter on The Raven's secure channels.

"They're regrouping," Aidan said, his voice tense as he leaned over the screens. "Donovan's pulling his forces together for one last strike. He knows he's cornered."

James nodded, his expression grim. "We need to be ready. He's going to come at us with everything he's got."

The group had anticipated this. They knew Donovan wouldn't go down without a fight, and they had prepared for this moment. Each of them armed and positioned strategically around their hideout, they braced themselves for the inevitable confrontation.

Sophie, crouched near a window with her weapon ready, glanced over at Aidan. "You know, if we survive this, I might actually miss the adrenaline rush."

Aidan chuckled, though the tension in his eyes remained. "If we survive this, I'm taking a long, boring vacation somewhere sunny."

"Deal," Sophie replied, her grip tightening on her weapon as she scanned the darkening horizon.

Donovan's Last Move

The attack came just as the last light of day disappeared. The sound of engines roaring in the distance grew louder, signalling the approach of Donovan's forces. Within moments, the quiet streets erupted into chaos as The Raven's men descended on their location.

The first shots rang out, shattering the stillness of the evening. Bullets tore through the air, hitting the brick walls and shattering windows. The group returned fire with precision, each of them falling into the rhythm of battle, their adrenaline surging.

Aidan, crouched behind a heavy oak table, worked furiously to keep the defensive systems online. He activated remote charges he had placed earlier, causing controlled explosions that rocked the building and sent debris flying, forcing Donovan's men into exposed positions.

"Keep them pinned!" Aidan shouted over the gunfire, his voice steady despite the chaos around him.

Evelyn, positioned on the second floor, used her vantage point to pick off the attackers with cold precision. Her hands were steady, her breath controlled as she squeezed the trigger, each shot a calculated strike.

"They're flanking us!" Sophie called out, spotting movement on the security cameras Aidan had set up earlier. Without hesitation, she grabbed a grenade from her belt, pulled the pin, and lobbed it toward the approaching group. The explosion was deafening, the force of it shaking the ground beneath them.

"Good one!" James shouted, reloading his weapon as he moved to cover Aidan, who was still deep in his work. James had been in firefights before, but this was different—this was personal. Every shot he fired, every man he took down, was a step closer to ending Donovan's reign.

But Donovan wasn't a man to be easily defeated. Emerging from the shadows, he moved with a deadly grace, his presence commanding the attention of both his men and his enemies. He was clad in tactical gear, a heavy rifle slung over his shoulder, and a cruel smirk on his lips.

"James!" Donovan's voice rang out, cutting through the chaos like a knife. "I knew you were behind this. You think you can take me down? You're just as weak as your father was."

James's blood boiled at the mention of his father. He broke cover, firing a burst of shots in Donovan's direction. Donovan dodged with practiced ease, returning fire as he moved closer.

The two men clashed in the centre of the room, the gunfire around them fading into a distant roar as they engaged in hand-to-hand combat. James swung first, his punch connecting with Donovan's jaw, sending the older man reeling.

But Donovan recovered quickly, countering with a swift knee to James's gut, doubling him over. Donovan grabbed James by the collar, hauling him up and slamming him against the wall with brutal force.

"You've always been a disappointment," Donovan snarled, his grip tightening. "Just like your father."

James gritted his teeth, fighting through the pain. He reached for the knife strapped to his ankle, pulling it free and slashing it across Donovan's arm. Donovan hissed in pain, but the momentary distraction was enough for James to break free.

He delivered a savage elbow to Donovan's face, feeling the satisfying crunch of bone. But Donovan, fuelled by rage and desperation, wasn't finished. He drew his own knife, lunging at James with deadly intent.

The two men grappled, the knives flashing in the dim light as they struggled for control. James's world narrowed to the fight in front of him—every breath, every move was focused on bringing Donovan down.

While James and Donovan fought, the rest of the group was locked in their own brutal battles. Aidan and Sophie worked in tandem, their movements synchronized as they held off the waves of attackers. Sophie's shotgun roared with each pull of the trigger, cutting down any who dared approach their position.

"Aidan, on your left!" Sophie shouted, spinning to take down a Raven enforcer who had managed to slip through their defences.

Aidan reacted instantly, firing a burst from his pistol that dropped the attacker before he could get any closer. He wiped the sweat from his brow, glancing at Sophie with a grin. "Still got my back, I see."

"Always," Sophie replied, her eyes scanning the room for the next threat.

Upstairs, Evelyn was running low on ammunition, her sniper rifle lying discarded as she switched to her sidearm. She could hear the shouts and gunfire below, but she remained focused, picking off the remaining men who tried to flank them from behind.

"They're thinning out!" Evelyn called down to the others, her voice steady despite the carnage around her. "But we need to finish this, now!"

The Final Blow

Back on the ground floor, the fight between James and Donovan

had reached a fever pitch. Both men were bloodied and exhausted, but neither was
willing to back down. Donovan swung his knife in a wide arc, aiming for James's throat, but James ducked, the blade slicing through the air just above his head.

With a burst of adrenaline, James drove his shoulder into Donovan's midsection, slamming him against a pillar. The impact forced the air from Donovan's lungs, and James took the opportunity to drive his knee into Donovan's stomach.

Donovan staggered back, clutching his ribs, but he still managed to smirk through the pain. "You think this ends with me?" he rasped. "There will always be another to take my place. You'll never be rid of men like me."

James stared at him, his chest heaving with exertion. "Maybe. But you won't live to see it."

With that, James lunged forward, knocking the knife from Donovan's hand and sending it skittering across the floor. He followed up with a series of brutal punches, each one fuelled by years of anger and pain. Donovan tried to fight back, but he was no match for James's fury.

Finally, with one last, savage punch, James sent Donovan crashing to the ground. The older man lay there, bloodied and broken, his smirk finally wiped from his face.

James stood over him, his chest heaving, his knuckles stained with blood. He could end it now, with one final blow, but instead, he stepped back, letting the weight of his victory sink in.

"You're done, Donovan," James said, his voice cold and final. "It's over."

Donovan tried to push himself up, but his strength was gone. He collapsed back onto the floor, the fight drained from him. The mighty Donovan Cross, the man who had terrorized the city for years, was finally defeated.

Aftermath and Reflection

As the police arrived, alerted by Evelyn's final call, the group stepped back, watching as Donovan was taken away in handcuffs. The fight was over, but the cost was high. They had survived, but they were forever changed by the events that had unfolded.

The sun was rising again, casting a pale light over the city as the group gathered one last time at their hideout. Exhausted but resolute, they reflected on what they had accomplished.

"It's finally over," Luke said, his voice filled with a mixture of relief and disbelief.

"No," James replied, shaking his head. "This is just the beginning. The city's still broken. We've got a lot of work to do."

"But this time," Evelyn added, her eyes meeting James's, "we do it on our terms."

Sophie, leaning against the wall, nodded. "No more running. No more hiding."

Aidan looked at his friends, feeling a sense of camaraderie he hadn't felt in years. "We stick together. We rebuild. And we make sure nothing like this ever happens again."

CHAPTER 23: A NEW DAWN

The sun rose slowly over Edinburgh, casting a golden hue across the city as it awoke from the chaos of the night before. The battle with Donovan was over, but the repercussions of that victory were only just beginning to ripple through the city. As the group emerged from their hideout, the exhaustion was evident on their faces, but so was a quiet sense of triumph.

Picking Up the Pieces

The streets were eerily quiet as they made their way back to the heart of the city. The usually bustling neighbourhoods were subdued, the shock of the revelations about Donovan and The Raven still sinking in. The city, once under the oppressive shadow of Donovan's control, was now on the brink of something new, something uncertain but hopeful.

James, Evelyn, Aidan, Sophie, and Luke walked together, the weight of their shared experience binding them in a way that words couldn't fully express. They had faced the darkness, and now they were stepping into the light, ready to rebuild what had been shattered.

"One question..", asked Luke as he stopped to readjust the bulky supplies holdall on his back, "Grenades?! The stories James used to tell me about you guys receiving covert tactical training.. I always thought James was taking the mick, now I dunno what to believe."

Aidan reached out and took the bag of Luke, a small smile tugging at his lips. Now wasn't the time, however Luke had proven he was capable of handling himself under pressure. The Agency would be impressed with the young man's grace under fire.

"We did it," Sophie murmured, almost as if she couldn't quite believe it.

"Yeah, we did. But there's still so much to fix.", Aiden's thoughts snapped back to the immediate future.

Evelyn's eyes scanned the city skyline, her thoughts already turning to what needed to be done. "Donovan might be gone, but his influence lingers. The corruption he fostered won't just disappear overnight."

James, ever the pragmatist, nodded in agreement. "We've got to clean up the mess. We can't just walk away from this."

The Search for Horace

As they approached the prison where Horace had been held, James felt a knot of anxiety tighten in his chest. The man who had been wrongfully accused and imprisoned for years was finally about to be free. The evidence they had uncovered had not only cleared his name but also revealed the extent of the conspiracy against him.

But as they arrived at the gates, the guards informed them that Horace had already been released. A sense of unease washed over the group.

"Released?" James asked, his voice tinged with disbelief. "When?"

"Just this morning," the guard replied, checking his records. "He left with a woman. Margaret, I think her name was."

"Margaret," Evelyn repeated, frowning. "Do we know her?"

Aidan shook his head, his mind already racing. "I'll check the prison's visitor logs. Maybe we can find out who she is."

Sophie, her instincts on high alert, looked at James. "Do you think he's in danger?"

James hesitated, his thoughts a jumble of possibilities. "I don't know. But we need to find him."

The group quickly mobilized, their relief at Horace's release now overshadowed by concern for his safety. Aidan accessed the visitor logs, pulling up the information on Margaret.

"She visited him regularly," Aidan said, scanning the records. "But there's not much else. No last name, no contact details."

Evelyn's mind was already piecing things together. "If she's someone close to Horace, she might have been helping him from the outside. But why didn't he tell us?"

James's jaw tightened. "Maybe he didn't want us involved. But we're not going to let him go off on his own."

As they searched for Horace, the group knew that their work wasn't finished. The city's institutions needed to be rebuilt, trust needed to be restored, and the people needed to feel safe again. They had taken down Donovan, but now they needed to ensure that his legacy didn't continue in his absence.

As they drove through the city, James spoke up, his voice low but determined. "We need to establish a special task force—one that operates with absolute integrity. We can't afford any leaks or corruption."

Evelyn nodded, her mind already racing with possibilities. "I know some people—officers and legal experts who haven't been compromised. We'll need to act quickly, though. We have to target the key players in The Raven's network simultaneously, so they can't warn each other."

James looked at Sophie. "You know the financial side better than anyone. Can you trace the money, find out where it's all hidden?"

Sophie's eyes narrowed with determination. "I can. We'll need to seize their assets, cut off their resources. Without money, they lose their power."

"Good," James replied. "And Aidan, you're our eyes and ears. We'll need you to monitor their communications, track their movements, and keep us ahead of them."

Aidan gave a small nod, his mind already working through the logistics. "I'll set up a secure network, one that can't be traced back to us. We'll need to move fast and hit them hard."

As they continued their search, Sophie turned to Evelyn. "We'll need to expose every dirty deal, every corrupt official who helped The Raven thrive. We can't let them rebuild."

Evelyn's eyes hardened. "I'll take care of it. I'll make sure the world knows what these people did—and that they pay for it."

Sophie's thoughts turned to the financial side of the operation. "There are accounts, shell companies, offshore assets. We need to freeze them all, redirect that money to rebuild the communities they destroyed."

James added, "And we'll need legal reforms. Stricter regulations, harsher penalties for corruption. Evelyn, your exposés can push lawmakers to make those changes."

Evelyn nodded, her resolve unwavering. "I'll make sure of it."

Luke, seated in the back, spoke quietly. "We have to help the people who were caught in the crossfire. The ones who were exploited, harmed by The Raven. They need support, not just financially, but emotionally."

James placed a hand on his brother's shoulder. "You're right. We'll set up programs—counselling, legal aid, financial assistance. They need to know they're not alone, that we're here to help them rebuild."

Luke looked out the window, his voice filled with quiet determination. "We can't let them down. We have to make sure they feel safe again."

Aidan's mind was already working on the technical side of things. "We need to secure the city's infrastructure. I'll develop surveillance and analytics systems that can detect any signs of new criminal networks before they can take root. And I'll work on cybersecurity protocols to protect our systems from being compromised again."

James looked at the group, his voice filled with conviction. "This city is ours now. We'll protect it, rebuild it, and make sure nothing like this ever happens again."

The Dawn of a New Era

As they cruised through the city streets, still on the lookout for Horace, the group found unexpected comfort in their work. They had faced the worst, yet here they were, still standing, still fighting. What they had built in the chaos—trust, loyalty, and an unbreakable bond—was stronger than ever.

That evening, as the sun dipped below the horizon, painting the sky in shades of orange and pink, they gathered at their old hideout. The place was filled with memories—good, bad, and everything in between. But now, it felt different. It wasn't just a hideout anymore; it was a reminder of what they had overcome.

"We've come a long way," Sophie said, her voice thoughtful as she glanced out over the city.

Aidan leaned against the wall, arms crossed. "Yeah, but we've got miles to go."

James chuckled, a rare sound from him. "And we'll get there—"

"Together!" Aidan, Sophie, and Evelyn cut in, grinning at the shared thought.

James shook his head, still smiling. "You guys are impossible."

They all laughed, the tension easing. The city lights flickered on below, one by one, and for the first time in a long while, they felt a sense of peace. They were bruised, battered, and far from perfect, but there was hope now. Maybe, just maybe, the scars would heal.

"We might be a mess," Evelyn said, her tone light but her meaning clear, "but we're still here."

"Damn right," Aidan agreed. "And if we can survive this, we can survive anything."

Sophie nodded. "Here's to the next fight, then."

James raised an imaginary glass. "To the next fight."

They stood there, watching the city breathe, and for a moment, the world felt still. They didn't need words to fill the silence—they had all the time in the world for that. Tonight, they just needed to be.

"Alright," Aidan finally said, pushing off the wall. "Let's get back to work. There's a city out there that still needs us."

And with that, they moved on, stepping into the night.

Printed in Great Britain
by Amazon